AMBUSH AT JUNCTION ROCK

Robert MacLeod

Young Link Conway wins some land in a poker game but has to risk his life to protect it against cattle baron Harry Peters. But his mind is not on the land. It's on Callie, the pretty saloon singer who turns out to be more trouble than poor Link wants to handle. After a near fatal duel and another close call with a bullet, Link decides it's time to make life a little more peaceful – even if it'll take a few more dead bodies to achieve it!

AMBUSH AT JUNCTION ROCK

Robert MacLeod

Curley Publishing, Inc.
South Yarmouth, Ma.

Library of Congress Cataloging-in-Publication Data

MacLeod, Robert, 1928–
   Ambush at Junction Rock / Robert MacLeod.—Large print ed.
    p. cm.
   1. Large type books. I. Title.
   [PR6061.N6A8 1991]
   823'.914—dc20
   ISBN 0–7927–0729–X (large print)   90–42469
   ISBN 0–7927–0730–3 (pbk.)   CIP

Published in Large Print by arrangement with Knightsbridge Publishing, Inc. in the United States, Canada, the U.K. and British Commonwealth and the rest of the world market.

Distributed in Great Britain, Ireland and the Commonwealth by CHIVERS LIBRARY SERVICES LIMITED, Bath BA1 3HB, England.

Printed in Great Britain

Another one for Laurie

AMBUSH AT JUNCTION ROCK

CHAPTER 1

I was so mad my hands were shaking, and I damn near let the carbine off again by accident.

Johnny Moore was scared. I couldn't tell if Joe Ochoa was or not – he was half Apache, and his face didn't show anything – but if he wasn't he should have been.

They shoved three cows and a calf back through the fence, where they'd cut it. "That's all of them," Johnny said.

The rest of the cows were already scattering out, back on syndicate land. Johnny looked kind of walleyed at me, where I stood beside my horse, covering the two of them with my Winchester. "You damn near shot me!" he said.

"I aimed to," I told him. "Don't know how I missed you."

"You'd kill me just 'cause a few syndicate

cows busted through your fence?"

"You cut the wire and pushed 'em through," I said. "More 'n fifty head. Now, to answer your question – and you be sure and tell Harry – yes, I'll shoot you, and any Development Land and Cattle Company hand or cow that crosses my line."

"What the hell's the matter with you? A whole section of good grass, and you won't use it nor lease it nor sell it. What the hell good does it do you?"

"All you gotta remember, Johnny, is it's *my* six hundred and forty, not yours, not Harry's, and not the syndicate's."

Joe said, "Let's go, Johnny." He put his horse through the fence where they'd pulled the four strands back on each side.

"What about our guns?" Johnny asked.

"He ain't gonna give 'em back. Come on."

I said, "Hold up. Fix the fence."

Johnny stepped down and led his horse through the gap. Joe got down, too, and they took their wire cutters, a hammer and staples, and fixed my fence.

I pitched their two six-guns down into the wash as far as I could throw them, into a hell of a tangle of catclaw and cactus. I said, "Come back and get 'em any time you get up enough nerve. But don't let me see you, 'cause I'll plug you!"

"It was Harry," Johnny said, "We had our orders, that's all."

"Johnny," I said, "when you're on my six hundred and forty, you ain't under Harry's orders, you're under this." I waggled my carbine.

Johnny said, "We do what he says, or we get fired."

"I can't figure out," I said, "what Harry thinks he'll get out of it. He's nothing but a foreman, working for wages like you. He figure they'll give him a partnership if he scares me into selling out?"

They mounted, and I guess Johnny figured I had cooled off. He got cocky again. He said, "We'll know that after he runs you off . . . 'cause that's exactly what he's gonna do. You'll sell cheap before he gets through with you."

I shoved my carbine into the saddle boot hanging on my rope horse, Sox, and picked up Johnny's where I'd dropped it. I shucked the cartridges out of it and looked around and saw a big stone half buried in the ground. I walked over to it and took his carbine by the barrel and swung it up over my head.

Johnny's voice went up high, and he yelled, "Hey! That's a brand new carbeen! Gimme that back!"

I swung it down twice and broke the stock

3

off clean, and kept hammering it on the stone till the receiver was all bashed up. Johnny was screeching at me all the time.

I didn't pay any attention to him. I said to Joe, "Who shot holes in the standpipe under my water tank, when I was down in Phoenix last month? Was that Harry's idea, or something you thought up yourself?"

He didn't say anything.

"What about the pump rod on my windmill, Joe? Who dropped it into my well? How come Harry ain't in on these little raids when I'm gone? Tough boy like him. Went charging up San Juan hill with Teddy Roosevelt. Tough enough to ramrod fifteen, twenty hardcases like you for the syndicate. Seems like he'd have the guts to come himself."

Johnny had his horse shoved right up against the barbwire, and was swearing and shaking his fist at me. I threw his busted carbine at him, and it went cartwheeling by about an inch from his face. He almost fell off his horse getting out of the way. That shut him up.

Joe said, "You'll get the idea one of these days, an' take what they offer, an' hit the trail outa here. You can't keep on buckin' the Development Land and Cattle Company by yourself."

4

He kicked his horse over to Johnny and got him by the sleeve and said, "Come on, you damn fool."

Johnny yelled at me, "You wait till Harry gets back! Just wait, that's all!"

"Where's he at?" I said. Johnny just went on cussing me, and I said, "Joe, where's Harry?"

Joe said, "He drove the buggy to Prescott. One of them owners is comin' from back east somewhere. Harry's gonna bring him out to headquarters."

"Pretty handy for Harry," I said. "Give him a good excuse not to come himself and cut my fence and shove those cows onto my grass. Did he think I might be home, this time?"

Joe reined his horse around. "Harry ain't scared of you, Link," he said. "Come on, Johnny," and they rode up the slope.

Johnny turned in his saddle and shook his fist again and yelled, "You stinkin' ragged-ass rawhider! Harry'll be over to see you!"

"I'll save him the ride," I said. "I'm going in and find him."

"Bull shit you are!" he yelled. "You better hunt you a hole to crawl in! From Harry! From me, too!"

I pulled my carbine out of the boot and took a rest against a fence post, and laid

5

one right under his horse. The gravel blasted up against its belly and it went straight up. Johnny went up still higher, turned over, and came down on his neck and shoulders. Joe gigged his horse and went over the hill. I watched Johnny lay there a while, then roll over and get up and rub the back of his neck.

His horse was pulling at the grass, and Johnny walked over to it. The horse held its head sideways so it wouldn't step on the reins, and trotted forty yards and went to grazing again. Johnny walked after it, and the same thing happened. They kept this up till they were over the hill. I could still hear him cussing the horse after they were out of sight.

Sox was boogered by the shooting and wanted to do some pitching when I got on him, but I talked him out of it and rode to my cabin. I got my blanket-lined coat, and headed for Prescott.

I hadn't cooled down any. The syndicate that owned the Development Land and Cattle Company sure wanted my one little section of ground. They'd bought up everything on three sides of it for miles around, and my six hundred and forty stuck into one side of their ground like a cinder in your eye. Not only that, it had good grass, a good well, and a big tank for watering stock. I'd had a couple of offers from them, and I sure wasn't going to try and ranch just one lone section. But this was my one chance to make a potful of money and quit cowboying – freezing all winter in somebody else's line camp, riding somebody else's fences, greasing somebody else's windmills, roping somebody else's calves and treating them for screwworms, and all for forty a month and found. They wanted that ground to sort of round things out, and give them a gate onto the road that ran along one side of my section. So I had them by the short hairs, and I was going to hold them up for all I could pry out of them.

I never was sure whether Harry Peters was just going ahead on his own, trying to spook me bad enough so I'd sell at their price. Maybe he was just trying to get in good, show himself real eager . . . and maybe he had his orders. Anyway, it was him doing the dirty work. Maybe if I was to threaten to take it to court, all this stuff Harry'd been trying, they'd settle on my terms, which they hadn't heard yet. Or maybe if I caught some syndicate cows through my fence again and dropped them for the buzzards and coyotes, they'd see they'd overplayed it.

I never had any use for Harry Peters, even before I won that section of land from Jay Connors, after I came down off the reservation in the fall two years ago. He had a

7

sour, tough-boy way about him that grated on me. Guess it was natural, him being foreman of an outfit that big, but it sure curried me the wrong way. He wasn't one of those gun-proud hardcases always looking for trouble, but he was tough enough. The thing was, though, I'd been in the war, like him, and I guess I'd been in as many brawls on Whisky Row as him, and I never was sure he could take me, if it ever came to that.

So I had two things on my mind right now. I was going to have it out with Harry Peters if I could find him in Prescott, and maybe I'd get a chance to talk face to face to the syndicate man Joe Ochoa said Harry was meeting at the train. Their offers to buy my place had come through Harry up to now. But Harry didn't have the authority to bargain. All he could do was tell me what they offered, and get sore when I laughed in his face.

It was fifteen miles to town, down out of the long slope of the valley under Mingus Mountain, then the road through that crazy, jumbled-up bunch of barn-size boulders they called Granite Dells, then the road past Fort Whipple. Sox had a way of going into a real smooth single-foot – like riding a rocking chair. He really covered the ground.

I got to thinking about what I'd do with a lot of money if I could pry it out of the syndicate owners. One thing, I'd sure quit cowboying. Maybe I'd go up on the Navajo Reservation a while, just lay around and enjoy it. It's funny how a certain place will pull at you.

When I went into the Army, I was just twenty. That was four years ago, in '98, and Bucky O'Neill was raising a cavalry outfit for Teddy Roosevelt's Rough Riders, to "Remember the Maine" and run those Spaniards out of Cuba. I guess every cowboy and miner in Arizona Territory wanted to go. I wound up working for Tom Horn, head packer for General Shafter, and the only fighting I saw was dragging mule loads of ammunition up to the troops just before they went up San Juan Hill. I heard a lot of slugs buzzing past, and watched the boys go up that hill, and all the smoke and yelling and racket. But, I never saw any Spaniards except dead ones, and a lot of dead Rough Riders, too. But maybe us packers saved the day, getting there in time with the ammunition, after that hangup getting it ashore. When the transport got there with all those mules and ammunition aboard, we couldn't get within a mile of shore, and there wasn't any docks or barges. It looked like old Four Eyes Roosevelt would have to call the whole thing off. But a mile of salt water didn't stop Tom Horn. He

9

said to shove those jugheads into the water, and that's what we did. Five hundred of them, and they swum ashore. We got the ammunition there in the ship's boats and began to pack it up the hill. I was under Lieutenant Horace Haverhill, from Boston. He didn't know the ass end of a mule from the front, but he sure got things organized, and us boys did the rest – me, Harry Peters, Jay Connors, and a lot of other good Arizona and New Mexico boys.

Well, when we were mustered out, Lieutenant Haverhill told me he and some others were coming out to Arizona for the Peabody Museum and dig up a big, old ruin up on the reservation – count the pots, arrowheads, and all that. He said they'd need somebody to run the camp and a string of pack mules for supplies, or maybe wagons, and asked me if I wanted the job. I sure did. In the Spring of 1900 I met them in Gallup, and, with four wagons and camp gear, we headed for Ram House Ruin, thirty miles northwest of Canyon de Chelly.

It was named Ram House Ruin because there was a big pictograph or petroglyph (I never got it straight which was which ... didn't even know those words, then) of a bighorn sheep on the cliff above the ruin, pecked into the rock with a stone.

10

I'd seen those prehistoric ruins all my life, but never paid much attention to them. They were all over Arizona Territory, little one-room buildings tucked away under a cliff overhang or great big ones like the one they called Montezuma's Castle in a limestone cliff near Camp Verde. That one is five stories high with twenty-five or more rooms a couple of hundred feet above the canyon floor. There were still parts of the old ladders that went from ledge to ledge to get into it, even though the scientists claimed it had been abandoned eight hundred years ago. The walls were part rock and part adobe brick, plastered over with adobe stucco. A modern bricklayer couldn't have done much better. The upper floors and the roof were held up by *vigas* cut from pine logs twenty inches in diameter. There wasn't any pine that size growing within fifty miles, and they didn't have any metal axes or saws . . . How they cut them and put them in place, nobody knows, any more than they know what made all those people pull up stakes and leave all of a sudden. The upper floors and roof were made of, first, a lot of poles laid side by side over the *vigas*, then a thick layer of brush crosswise to the *vigas*, then a foot or more of packed dirt almost as hard as concrete. Most of the rooms in the cliff dwellings, and even in the big surface

11

ruin called Tuzigoot on a hill near Clarkdale weren't connected to each other. They were small, maybe ten feet by twelve, with a fire pit, a thin slab of rock upright in the floor inside the door to prevent drafts, and ventilation holes built high in the walls. Every room has a little rock-lined hole in the back called the *sipapu* – that's the entrance to the spirit world underground. The Hopi houses still have them. Every big ruin has a *kiva*, too, or more than one, a sacred room where they worshiped the gods and dressed for the dances. The Hopi villages still have those.

We found the kinds of things at Ram House Ruin that you find in most of the ruins. There were *manos* and *metates* for grinding corn, and a lot of pottery, mostly broken. Some of the big *ollas* would have held thirty gallons. There were arrowheads, spearheads, stone drills, arrow straighteners and axes, a few rotting yucca-fiber sandals, and some ragged pieces of woven cloth with very fine designs. There were mummies, too . . . not embalmed, just dried out. They were usually buried in the refuse heaps below the ruins, but sometimes under the floors in storage pits lined with slabs of rock. The bodies still had some meat and hair on them, and were usually doubled up and laid on their sides with little bowls of food and face paint. There were spears, arrows, and shell and turquoise jewelry with them. Most of them had their faces covered with a bowl which was always what the scientists called "killed," that is, it had a hole knocked in the bottom. In a storage room full of huge bowls of corn and seed, we found a bundled-up net used for hunting, very well made of yucca fiber and twisted human hair. It was six feet wide and almost two hundred feet long.

I came down to Prescott that winter, and went back in the summer of 1901 . . . it was the best job I ever had. I learned a lot about those old Anasazis that built Ram House twelve hundred years ago, and found out those Boston greenhorns were all right and knew what they were doing. That country really got under my hide – the quiet, the land that just went on forever, and those canyons I couldn't even describe. I liked the Navajos, too. They'd had about as raw a deal from the government and the Bureau of Indian Affairs as any Indians you ever heard of – the Cheyennes, the Nez Percé and all them. They were dirt poor, on the worst land you could imagine for making a living. But they were proud and dignified. They didn't trust any white man much except the traders that talked Navajo and had been there for years, like the Hubbells at Ganado and

13

the Wetherills near Kayenta. And they were riders, believe me!

Anyway, I was sorry when the job was over. I came back to Prescott and went to work for the Development Land and Cattle Company, where Harry Peters was foreman. Jay Connors worked there, too. His father had homesteaded the ranch, but he had drank half of it away, and Jay Connors finished the job, all except that one section where he lived like a hog in that two-room cabin. I can look back now, and see how Harry Peters was trying to get him to sell to the syndicate even then, and sure didn't help him to quit the boozing.

I crossed Harry up, though, by getting in that stud game in the Palace Bar. I had my pay from the dig on the reservation, and a couple of months wages from the syndicate, and Harry and I both sat in the game. Jay was drunk as usual, and getting drunker. I thought it was funny when Harry kept raising Jay on about every hand, and then if Jay would drop out, Harry'd like as not drop out, too, and didn't seem to care if somebody else took the pot. That is, not till Jay was broke. Then Harry said why didn't he put up his section of land. Well, Jay did, all or nothing on one hand. Harry caught queens full of aces . . . but I drew two eights to three kings, and Jay only had a busted flush. I picked up a hundred fifty dollars of Harry's money, and the section of land. Harry made me an offer for it right after the game. He got real friendly and said the syndicate would pay high for it, maybe five hundred dollars, and he'd see I had a steady job there for as long as I wanted. I told him five hundred wasn't even openers in that game, and he could go chase his tail (only that wasn't exactly what I recommended). Then I quit before he could fire me, and moved onto my section. That's when he started crowding me, and every time he did something to scare me off, my price went up and I got madder. He should've figured me out better than he did.

I rode down Gurley Street about one in the afternoon, past all the burnt out buildings from the fire back in 1900. It wiped out five whole blocks . . . the bank, the livery barns, the stores, cathouses, and Whisky Row. The fire hadn't even cooled down before they had the faro and poker games going, and a plank bar set up in the Court House plaza. Even the bank was back in business before the week was out. By now, they'd most all been rebuilt.

I rode out of my way to go past the depot. The train was late, so the syndicate man wasn't here yet. I rode up Montezuma Street, and tied up in front of the Palace Bar. Harry Peters' buggy was there.

I tied Sox at the hitchrack and went in. It was so dark, after the sun's glare outside that I couldn't see a thing. I leaned against the wall beside the batwing doors till things began to come clear, like they were appearing out of a fog.

Bill Monahan was stooped down behind the bar, broaching a barrel of beer, to judge from the sound. There was a three-hand stud game going on at one of the back tables. Callie was walking around somebody sitting at the faro table, heading for the casekeeper's chair. She used to keep the case for "Ruby" Blair sometimes, when she wasn't singing or having a drink with one of the customers. For once the sight of her didn't do anything funny to my insides the way it always did before. I hardly even saw her, because Harry Peters was sitting there with his chair tipped back, his Stetson pulled down over his eyes, and that damn rust-color hair hanging down over the freckles on his red neck. His back was to me. It looked like he was killing time till the train got in by bucking the tiger.

Ruby Blair wasn't there. We called him Ruby because of the walnut-sized ruby ring on the little finger of his right hand that shone like a red whorehouse light under the overhead lamp. Callie said, "I called him, Harry. He'll be here in a minute."

As she went past Harry, he put out his arm and grabbed her around the rump and hauled her up against him. I started to grin, waiting for her to backhand him across the face. Her job, besides singing, was to be nice to the customers, and have a drink with them if they wanted; and when some drunk got out of line and started pawing her, she'd always turn it off without making him mad or hurting his feelings. But, if they were sober and tried anything raw, she'd swing on them with her hand or a bottle or anything close by.

Only this time, she didn't. She took a quick look around and saw that Monahan was still down behind the bar, and the stud players weren't looking. She never even looked my way. She hugged Harry's head to her for a minute, knocking his hat sideways, then pushed away and said, "Here comes Ruby."

She sat in the casekeeper's chair, and Ruby Blair came out of the back room in his striped pants, white shirt, string tie, and flowered vest. The green eyeshade hid the top of his face under his slicked-down hair so you couldn't see his little, squinched-up, black eyes. He smoothed his longhorn mustache, sat down, shuffled the cards and put them in the box, and said, "Hello, Harry. How's the campaign going?"

"What campaign?" Harry said. Then, he laughed and said, "I think he's starting to get the message. Johnny Moore and Joe Ochoa warmed things up a little this morning, at least, they had their orders."

It all boiled up in me again – the standpipe shot out from under my water tank, my stovepipe stuffed with a sack and smoking me out of my cabin, the rifle shot smashing my window that night two weeks ago, and this morning, Johnny Moore and Joe Ochoa cutting my fence, and shoving those cows onto my place.

I walked up behind him, and Ruby Blair scowled up at me. Callie gave me that big smile and said, "Why, Link! What are you doing here this time of day?"

Harry started to turn his head, but I grabbed a handful of his hair and hauled him right over backward, chair and all. His feet hooked under the table and dumped it over, with the case box, cards, coppers, money, Harry's beer, and everything falling onto Ruby Blair.

Harry hit the floor on his shoulders, cussing a blue streak, and rolled over onto his knees getting a foot tangled in the chair rungs. He raised up and when he was about half standing, I swung one from the floor square on his mouth and dumped him on his back again. He rolled over onto his hands and knees, and when he was half up to his feet, I hit him again. This time he pitched onto his face and laid there. I hoped he'd stay down. I didn't know if I could hit him again right-handed, because my hand felt like I broke it.

He finally got up and his eyes looked funny. He had the guts, though. He didn't go for his gun like I thought he might, but he took a feeble swing at me. I hit him with my left fist, and he staggered backward ten feet and fell up against the wall.

Everybody was there by then, hollering at me and milling around. Callie grabbed my left arm and said, "Link, you stop this! What's got into you?"

Well, I didn't want her to get hurt. I stepped back and picked up my hat. Harry was still on his feet, but only the wall was holding him up. His mouth was a bloody mess. I stood there rubbing my right fist, and Ruby Blair said, "Bill, throw the son of a bitch out!"

I swung around on him and said, "It's your idea, you do it, Ruby!"

Bill Monahan said, "Now everybody calm down! Link, what the hell is the matter with you?"

19

"Ask Harry," I said. "And pour me a drink."

"You didn't give him much chance," Callie said.

"I won't next time, either," I told her.

Ruby and Monahan got Harry over to a chair, and Monahan got a wet bar towel and swabbed off his face. Harry shoved his hand away and tried to get up, but he couldn't make it, and sat back. He looked up at me, and there wasn't any expression on his face at all. He spoke kind of thick, with his mouth busted up that way. He said, "Link, if you're smart, you'll leave the Territory."

"You'd better take your own advice," I told him. "Did you really think you could set your hands to breaking my pump, throwing shots through my window, cutting my fence, and shoving syndicate cows onto my place, and I wouldn't do anything about it? Now, I'm gonna tell you! Anything that belongs to the syndicate that moves onto my place, I'll shoot it. And that goes for cows and cowhands ... and specially you, Harry. And if you want some more of what you just got, you don't have to come looking, just send word."

Up till then, nobody had noticed the man that had come in and was standing just inside the door. He was well dressed, had on a derby, and was carrying a satchel. He walked over, pushing Monahan aside, looked down at Harry, and shook his head. Then he looked at me and said, "You must be Conway."

I was pretty sure who he was, but I asked, "Who the hell are you?"

"I'm Moyers," he said. "Development Land and Cattle. When Harry didn't meet the train, they told me at the depot I'd find him here."

"Well, you found him. You can have him."

I turned away to go to the bar and get my drink, but he caught my sleeve and said, "Just a minute. Is it true, what you were saying? About all that . . . that persecution? Has Harry been doing that?"

"And you don't know a damn thing about it!" I grinned at him. "Why don't you ask him?"

He turned back to Harry. "Harry?" he said.

Harry said, "Well, God damn it, you wanted his section, didn't you?"

Mr. Moyers shook his head slowly. "You fool! You stupid fool! It'll cost us double, now!"

I said, "Maybe more than that, Mr.

21

Moyers. I might've listened to something reasonable, before. But you sure got my back up. I'm gonna see Judge Hamilton. I figure I got a pretty good law case."

"Listen, Conway!" he said. "You can't make out, ranching just one section. You never meant to. You're just out to hold us up for a piece of ground that didn't cost you a cent. It's true, isn't it? You did win it in a poker game?"

"What's the difference how I got it? I got it."

"Of course you're bluffing about shooting anybody that comes onto your place," Moyers said, "so start talking sense."

"When you get out to headquarters, ask Johnny Moore how close he came to getting shot this morning."

He looked at me a long time. Then he sighed and said, "What's your price?"

"Ten dollars an acre. Six hundred and forty acres."

He winced like something had bit him. "Now let's be reasonable!"

I shoved him aside and walked out. It wasn't till I untied Sox and climbed into the saddle that he came out and asked, "You've got a deed to that section?"

"Over in the bank, in their safe."

"You'll sign a quit claim?"

22

"Soon as you sign the check."

We went to the bank which handled the legal stuff for the syndicate. They made out a deed, and I signed it.

I will never forget one little detail of the check Moyers gave me. I'd never in all my life made more than forty a month and found, and now I held that little piece of paper in my hand. It had "The Arizona Bank, Prescott, Arizona Territory" printed on top, "Development Land and Cattle Company" on the bottom and up in the right-hand corner, "November sixth, 1902." In between it said, "Pay to the Order of Lincoln L. Conway – Six Thousand Four Hundred and 00/100 — Dollars."

Moyers said, "Get your stuff out of the cabin tonight, will you? I don't want any more trouble out there. Look, Conway, could you see your way clear to leave town? You've got the money to go anywhere you want to, now."

"Burn the cabin down if you want to. I'm not going back out there. And about leaving town, well, I'll think it over. I don't want to kill anybody. And I don't want Harry hunting my hide, either."

He went out.

I opened an account for six thousand three hundred dollars, got a hundred in cash, went and hired a room in the Brinkmeyer Hotel, and put Sox in the livery barn.

If anything ever called for a celebration, this did! I went back to the Palace Bar.

CHAPTER 2

I'd seen a lot of wild nights along Whisky Row, from the Kentucky Bar to the Depot House, "forty drinks below," as we said, but I guess my party or brawl or spree or whatever you want to call it sort of set a mark. The Cabinet House and the Palace Bar were the stockmen's hangouts, and we had the Palace rocking on its foundations that night.

24

It started slow. I was a little nervous that maybe Harry Peters would be there with some of the syndicate hands to get even with me ... but he wasn't. There were only half a dozen at the bar, and a few at the faro and poker tables.

Callie came over to me and put her arm through mine and said, "Did he buy you out?"

"For cash. We're gonna howl tonight!"

"I hope you held out for a good price," she said, and when I told her, "Let's have a drink," she said, "I hope you aren't carrying that money on you!"

"It's in the bank, all but enough for a little celebration."

I put fifty dollars on the bar and told Monahan, "Let me know when it runs out, and don't turn anybody down!"

He took it and grinned, and said, "First one's on the house, Link! What's yours?" But he knew what mine was, and poured me a double Jim Beam, and Callie took a small port wine. By then, the gamblers had quit the games and came over to the bar, grinning, and were shaking my hand. Even Ruby Blair came over when the faro players quit, and said, "Congratulations, Link. I hope you nailed 'em good. How much did Moyers give you?"

25

"Enough to pay for a party. Have a drink."

The boys kept Monahan jumping, pouring the drinks, and one of his late shift bartenders came in to help. The boys started yelling for Callie to sing.

I wouldn't want anybody to get a wrong idea about Callie, or any of the girl singers in the saloons. They weren't hookers. The hookers were all in the cribs and houses in the "restricted" area, which, believe me, wasn't restricted so far as what went on down there. The singers, like Callie, were entertainers, and no more. They gave tone to a place, and on summer nights, even the Prescott people who'd die before they went into a saloon used to sit on the benches in the plaza across Montezuma Street, just to hear the girls sing. Some of them, like Callie, had real good voices.

They boosted her up and she sat on the bar. The piano player hit a couple of chords, and she sang, "There'll be a Hot Time in the Old Town Tonight." Everybody cheered because that was the favorite song of the Spanish-American War, and just right for my celebration, too. She sure looked pretty, just a little thing with a real nice figure, big blue eyes, and yellow hair. I guess her dress was pretty scandalous, according to what the Prescott housewives wore. The skirt hit her

26

about half way up the calf of her leg instead of dragging on the ground, and you could even see a couple of lace petticoats. Her arms were bare, too, and her collar cut low so when she bent over you could see down her front. But believe me, nobody ever laid a hand on her, because she was a lady, and you knew it right away when you looked at her. Not only that, but Monahan and his bartenders would have caved in your skull with a bung starter if you got fresh. And I guess Ruby Blair was maybe in love with her, because he watched her close, and he had picked a couple of fights with boys that wanted to dance with her or buy her a drink. Him and Monahan argued over it sometimes, because she was supposed to have a drink with the customers once in a while. Anyway, they said Ruby had killed two men down in Tucson at different times – some arguments over his faro layout – and that would make the boys think twice before they tried to put a hand on her where they shouldn't, or anything like that.

Then she sang, "Tenting Tonight, Tenting on the Old Camp Ground," and some of the boys were sniffling and wiping their eyes. When she ended with "Nita, Juanita," a couple of them were really bawling in their drinks. I hadn't ever told anybody, specially not her, but every time I'd seen her in the

27

year she'd been in Prescott, I got a funny choked-up feeling. I'd've asked her to marry me if I thought I had any chance.

When she went to get down off the bar, she held out her arms to me, and I got my hands on her waist. They went all the way around. When she jumped down, she sort of fell into my arms for a minute and her hair was against my mouth. She felt soft against me, and smelled like lavender. She stayed there just a second, smiling up at me, then moved away and began to fuss with her hair.

Things got pretty wild and confused. More girls had come in, some of them from the line, and the boys were dancing with them and with each other because there weren't enough girls to go around. My knees were wobbly and my head buzzing, and I sat down at one of the poker tables. The boys kept coming up to congratulate me and I had to drink with all of them.

Then Monahan came over and said the fifty dollars was all drunk up, and I got the other fifty out of my wallet and Callie came up and said, "No, Link! You mustn't throw your money around. Here, let me keep it for you," and took the money.

"Callie, this is a celebration, and I got a lot more than this over in the bank. Give it to

28

him." She laughed, and said, "All right, you big silly!" and handed Monahan the money.

She said, "But, Link, now that you've got a stake, don't let it slip through your fingers. You invest it somewhere."

"Don't worry. I'm gonna buy a business or something. No more cowboying for me! Callie, you need any money? Come on, we'll go over to the bank and get you a handful!" And I meant it. She was the prettiest little thing I'd ever seen, and I was crazy about her.

"You know I wouldn't take money from you, or any man. And anyway, even if I would, the bank is closed, silly. But you're awful sweet!" And she patted my cheek.

I grabbed her, pulled her onto my lap and kissed her. She shoved away looking over her shoulder, and got up in a hurry. Somebody came bulling through the dancers and backhanded me across the face with a full arm swing that shook me up.

And there was Ruby Blair in front of me, with a snarl on his face. "On your feet, you son of a bitch!"

I got half out of the chair, and he hit me and knocked me back, and everybody came crowding around. I got my foot in his belly and shoved, and he went back a couple of steps. That gave me a chance to get up. The girls were squealing and Callie was yelling, *"Ruby! No!"* Monahan and his bartender came charging out from behind the bar.

Ruby sure didn't know anything about fist fighting. He came in swinging wild and, drunk as I was, I caught him right on the chin. He pitched full length onto his face. I thought I'd really busted my hand this time. It ached clear to my shoulder. He laid there a minute, then rolled over and got onto his knees.

The boys were holding Monahan and his bartender back, and yelling at me to kick Ruby in the face. He had a gun on his hip, like all the rest of us, and he was snarling and spitting like a bobcat when he went for it. I made a grab for mine and fumbled it, but somebody grabbed his arm and somebody else got his gun. They grabbed him by the collar and the seat of his pants, turkey-walked him to the door, and slung him out onto the street.

They got me up on their shoulders and marched me around the saloon and set me down belly to the bar, and we all cheered my victory and had some more drinks.

Things got fuzzier after that, and the last I remember was somebody trying to hold me up and steer me down the street to the hotel.

CHAPTER 3

I woke up in bed in my room, with the sun glaring through my eyelids and my head this big, and my stomach slowly turning over and over. Somebody had undressed me down to the hide. I groaned, and somebody said, "How do you feel, Link?"

I rolled onto my side and there was Callie in bed with me! I squeezed my eyes shut and thought a while. I thought I'd been so drunk I was seeing things. I looked again, and, my God, it *was* her! She was sitting up and smiling down at me, and she didn't have a stitch on her, either.

I wanted to crawl into a hole somewhere. I was too embarrassed to look at her again, and I thought, my God, now you've done it!

She slid down onto her side and got her arms around my neck and hugged me. I said, "My God, Callie! I wouldn't've . . . why, I never had the nerve to even lay a hand on you! And now . . ."

She had her face pushed into the hollow

of my neck. "Link, you think I'd be here in bed with you if I didn't want to? Wild horses couldn't drag me into bed with a man I didn't like!"

"You really mean that? I didn't insult you or make you come with me, or anything? Because, Callie, my God, I wouldn't ever try anything with you!"

"You were drunker than I thought. Don't you remember it at all? Me helping you home, so nobody could take advantage of you or rob you on the street? You don't remember telling me you love me and want to marry me? Why, Link! I believed you! I wouldn't be here if I thought you didn't love me! Oh, I'm so ashamed!" and she started to get out of bed.

I grabbed her and pulled her back. "Wait! I don't remember a damn thing after that fight with Ruby. But, listen, whatever I said, I meant it! I do love you! I'm crazy about you!"

She kissed me then and cuddled up to me, and said, "Well, I knew all night you were too far gone to . . . well, I mean, I loved just lying there beside you and hugging you."

Those were the most wonderful words I ever heard. She was so much a lady and so kind of above me, and I never had the faintest idea she liked me any more than a dozen others . . . she was just nice to all of us, in a business way. So now, when she began to fool around, I was shocked, but more excited than I'd ever been in my life . . . and you bet I wasn't thinking about Harry Peters or my money or anything else right then.

Anyway, after while we just laid there with our arms around each other, and I said, "You really mean you'll marry me?"

"I don't know, Link. Maybe I would, but we have to be sensible. I make pretty good money at the Palace, but you haven't got a job any more. And maybe I sound kind of hard, but I won't ever marry a forty-a-month cowboy. I couldn't ever live like that, and it wouldn't last either."

"Now, wait a minute. I'm no forty-a-month cowboy any more. I've got money. A lot of money. We could go anywhere we wanted and live like we wanted."

"Ruby said they'd give you maybe a thousand dollars for your section, and that wouldn't last us long."

"Ruby's a damn fool. Moyers paid me ten dollars an acre. I got sixty-three hundred dollars in the bank!"

"Why, Link! Why, that's wonderful!" She swarmed all over me again, and kissed me a dozen times.

When I got my breath back, I said, "So I'm gonna buy a business somewhere, maybe a gun shop or a hardware store. I was going

33

to take a little vacation, maybe up on the reservation, but now I won't waste time. We'll get married, and I'll start looking for just what we want."

She got real serious then. "Link, you were awful drunk last night, and you're hung over pretty bad, and not thinking straight right now with me in your arms. I won't say yes or no yet, just maybe. You take some time and think it over, then if you're sure, why you ask me again, and we'll see."

She kissed me and propped herself on one elbow and looked down at me. "I always thought you were good looking, but I never knew your eyes were so blue! Or your hair so black. If it wasn't for that broken nose, you'd be handsome! All those muscles, and no fat on you!"

Well, then, I had to tell her how beautiful she was ... all pink and white and round, and that long yellow hair. I made her stand up so I could see how long it was, and it hung down to her round little bottom. She really was beautiful, and I wanted to marry her and love her and take care of her forever.

She got back into bed and propped her chin on her hand and looked at me a while. Then she said, "Somehow I can't picture you running a hardware store."

"Well, I just said that. I haven't had time to

figure it out, but I'll think of something. One thing sure, I've got my big chance now, and I'm never gonna work for somebody else."

"You used to talk all the time about the reservation. That job you had up there, you liked that, didn't you?"

"That country really pulls at me. It's so damn big, and those white clouds sailing in the bluest sky you ever saw, room to move, no damn Harry Peters yelling at you ... I can't tell you ... I guess I don't even understand it myself. But there's nothing up there for me, nothing for a white man except maybe a trading post. And the government only allows so many, and you have to have a license and all that."

"I was born up there. Lived there till I was sixteen."

"You never told me. Where was that?"

"I never thought you'd be interested. Did you ever hear of the Ram House Trading Post?"

"Why, that's up near Canyon de Chelly. That's where we got our supplies and mail, when I was packer on that dig. Lieutenant Haverhill, he was my boss in the army, him an' some other Boston rich men ran the dig up at Ram House Ruin. Old Man Beasley had the trading post, fifteen miles from the ruin. You mean you lived up there?"

35

"You remember the Evangelical Mission, near the trading post?"

"The building. But it was falling to pieces. The sign was still on it."

"My father built it. Reverend Allison. Only he wasn't a reverend, he wasn't ordained. He was just crazy in the head. Trying to preach hell-fire to the Navajos – drinking, adultery, gambling – they didn't have the slightest notion what he was talking about. They thought he was funny in the head, but they were always kind to him because they think a crazy man is some kind of magic. They used to give us corn and meat, and all the old man did was rave at them and tell them they were going to hell. Well, he wasn't funny to me! Nor to my mother, either. She ran away when I was ten. Couldn't stand him or that place any longer. And he blamed me. Said I was wild and bad, and it was God's judgment. He'd catch me hanging around the trading post talking to Old Man Beasley, and he said Beasley was a dirty old man with lustful thoughts. Old Beasley never looked at me sideways. Too old and too crippled up with rheumatism, for one thing. And when my father'd catch me talking to some nice Navajo boy, he'd beat me black and blue with a strap."

"The old bastard!" The thought of anyone

laying a strap on that beautiful behind of hers had me boiling inside.

"Well, I couldn't stand it, either. He took me to a revival meeting in Phoenix, and we heard Billy Sunday raving about 'Come to Jesus.' A lot of stupid people went crawling down the aisle and confessed a lot of sins. And my father told me to confess my lying, disobedience, rebellious spirit and my fornication with the unenlightened savages. I ran out of that tent and never went home again."

"What ever happened to him?"

"I don't know. I guess when he couldn't make any headway with the Navajos, he got discouraged. Anyway, he just pulled up stakes a couple of years later, I heard, and I don't know if he's alive or dead. And I don't care!"

"What did you do? How did you live?"

"Well, I didn't have any real education, except my mother taught me to read and write, and my father made me learn the Bible. I had to read it end to end, once a year. But that wasn't any good for making a living. I tell you it wasn't easy to be a good girl, but I waited tables and did housework. Then I found out I had a pretty good voice, and I got to singing in the saloons. This is the best job I've ever had. Bill Monahan really looks after his girls. He's like a father to us. And Ruby never lets anybody even get near me."

"What about Ruby? Why'd he get so damn mad when I just kissed you on the cheek?"

"Oh, he's in love with me. It's pretty tiresome. Reminds me of my father . . . just like him. Always lecturing me and getting mad if anyone looks at me. But there's no harm in him, Link."

"No harm! Hell, he was going to shoot me!"

"Oh, he wouldn't have, really. He thought he was protecting my honor or something. He was only trying to scare you."

"So you were born up there on the reservation! You talk Navajo, and all that?"

"Just like English, and I know all about running a trading post. I did it for Old Man Beasley a lot of times when his rheumatism got him down. That's what got me thinking . . ." her voice trailed off, and she laid there looking thoughtful, staring up at the ceiling.

"Thinking what?"

"Well, about you and what you're going to do with your money. And knowing how much you like it up there on the reservation."

I waited while she thought some more, and then she said, "How'd you like to run a trading post up there?"

I had thought about it, but I knew there

38

was no chance of anything like that. But now I began to get excited. That would let me live up there for good, somewhere on the reservation, and make a good living too. It would exactly fill the bill for me.

"I think Old Man Beasley would sell the Ram House Trading Post. He's been there thirty years, now, he's sixty-five or more, and the winters nearly kill him off, with his rheumatism so bad. He hardly ever sees a white man, and he has to depend more and more on Navajo help to run the post and drive to Gallup for supplies. And if I know Navajos, they steal him blind, and he knows it and can't do anything about it."

"Why that's wonderful! That's just exactly what I want!"

"Now don't get all excited. It's just a thought I had. But I think it's worth a try, if it's really what you want."

"How much would it cost?"

"I don't know. You can't own the building, you know. It's on reservation property. All you can own is the license and your own stock. But it's just the same as owning it, really, because if you run a good post and the Navajos like you and you don't cheat them too much or sell them liquor, there's no trouble getting your license renewed every year. I know all about that post . . . I'm sure it's just the way it was seven years ago, last time I was there. I think the stock would be worth seven or eight thousand dollars, but I bet Old Man Beasley would grab at five thousand. And now would be the time, because every year he used to swear he'd never stay another winter, but was going to retire to California and bake his old bones in the sun."

"I'll leave tomorrow!" Then I thought of something, and I said, "But, listen. I don't speak a dozen words of Navajo. I couldn't run the post."

"Well, if he'll sell to you, I've got a lot of good friends up there, Navajo boys I used to know, that went to school and learned English. You could hire one of them. I'll write to a couple of them when it's time."

Then she rolled over and pushed against me and hugged me, and whispered into my ear, "And you never can tell, maybe you'll find a nice, white wife that talks Navajo."

My headache was sure gone by now. I pulled her closer.

After a while she said, "You'll have to take cash when you go. Wave five thousand dollars cash under the old man's nose, and I bet he'll fall for it. But take all your money, in case he's a hard bargainer. A check wouldn't impress him near as much."

I was pulled two ways. I hated to get out of that bed, but I was all in a sweat to get started for Ram House Trading Post, deep in the reservation in the middle of those endless plains and huge rock cliffs. It wasn't too far from the Grand Canyon, which I'd never seen, and only thirty miles from Canyon de Chelly, that people said was the most beautiful place in the world. I knew I couldn't settle down till I'd either bought the post or not bought it, and I had to get it settled.

I watched Callie dress . . . all those underpants, and camisoles, and corset covers, and corsets, and then that spangled, red party dress. It was a shame to see that pretty little body of hers get covered up with layer after layer.

She said she wouldn't go to the Chop House with me for breakfast – it was almost lunch time, anyway – but she said she'd try to see me before I left.

Under all the excitement – her sleeping with me, and the chance to buy a trading post, and maybe even marry her – one thing still nagged at my mind. I was afraid she'd be sore, but I had to find out. "Callie, are you maybe kind of soft on Harry Peters? You were sore at me when I slugged him, and before that, he was pawing you and it didn't look to

41

me like you minded very much."

"What?" and she was really puzzled. Then she said, "Oh, you mean at the faro table. Listen . . . he loses a lot of money to Ruby, and Ruby gives me a percentage when I bring somebody to the table. Sure, he tries to get smart, like all the rest of you . . . but if you think for one minute it goes any farther . . . if you can't trust me after last night . . . why then, Link . . ."

"Aw forget it. You sure can't expect me not to be jealous. See you tonight at the Palace Bar."

"Better not, Link. Ruby'll be there, and you handled him kind of rough last night. He's not one to forget a grudge, and we don't want anything to happen to spoil our plans, do we?"

That "we" had me walking about two feet off the ground, and I knew everything was going to come out exactly the way I wanted.

I ate lunch, then bought an oiled-silk money belt, and went to the bank to draw my money out. It's surprising how little room sixty-three hundred-dollar bills takes up, wrapped around your middle in a money belt.

I bought a tarp, two blankets, new Levi's, a couple of shirts, and some wool long johns. I got a gallon canteen, a box of crackers and some cheese, and two pounds of jerky. I had my 30.30 Winchester and a Colt's .45, and I got a box of shells for both. Everything would go in my saddlebags or in a roll behind my saddle. It would make a pretty big bundle, but not heavy, and old Sox could pack me and it all day and not raise a sweat. There'd be towns to stop in till I got on the reservation, and I didn't need any cooking gear.

I was so anxious to get started I almost left late that afternoon, but I knew I couldn't make it to Jerome that night. I'd have to camp up on Mingus Mountain. I could hardly stand it not to see Callie that night, but I got sensible again and had a late supper and went to my room. The whole town knew I had all that money, and the bank clerk would probably blab it around that I had got it out of the bank. Not only that, if I went to see her at the Palace Bar, I'd sure have a drink or two, and Ruby Blair would be there, and maybe even Harry Peters. Harry would be aching to get back at me, and he might bring Johnny Moore with him, looking for me. I just didn't dare risk anything happening to spoil my big chance – like maybe getting robbed.

I wasn't feeling too good, anyway, after that brawl last night. I went to bed early, figuring I'd get an early start. Well, I slept like I had died, and didn't wake up till about nine. By the time I ate and got Sox packed, it was after ten.

I rode up Montezuma Street and was going to tie up at the Palace Bar, and go in to say goodbye to Callie. Then I thought what's the use to ask for trouble . . . I'd see her soon, anyway . . . and I rode on.

I passed a buckboard and a twenty-mule freight rig, and two Army wagons from Fort Whipple before I went through Granite Dells and turned north toward Mingus Mountain. I was going to make a swing away from the road to pass wide around the section I sold to the syndicate, just so I wouldn't run into Harry Peters or Johnny Moore, but I couldn't bring myself to do that. Avoiding trouble any place where Callie was, was one thing, but damned if I'd ride a foot out of my way to dodge Harry Peters. I made sure the carbine was loose in the boot, and walked Sox up the road right past what used to be my gate. I could see smoke rising from the cabin over the hill, but not a sign of anybody around.

Then something made me look back, and there was Johnny Moore, sitting his horse in the gate, looking at me. I stopped Sox and swung him around and pulled my carbine out of the boot as he turned. I jacked a shell into the chamber, and held the carbine ready, but I didn't point it at Johnny.

44

He turned and went back through the gate like his tail was on fire. He was hunched over the saddlehorn with his face in the horse's mane, and he didn't stop to shut the gate. I heard him clattering off through the junipers back toward the cabin.

I rode on a few hundred yards and backed into the brush and waited for ten or fifteen minutes, thinking maybe he'd gone to fetch Harry Peters, but nothing happened, so I went on.

I had to climb the long switchbacks up Mingus Mountain, ten miles ahead, and then the long, twisting road down to Jerome, the copper mining town hanging onto the steep mountainside by its teeth, ten or fifteen miles the other side of Mingus. I'd get there late, but that didn't matter. I was on my way!

In about half an hour I passed a long, jerk-line freight rig that was hauling supplies to Jerome, and a couple of miles farther on, at the top of the first steep switchback, I stopped to let Sox blow.

I rolled a smoke, and was sitting there looking around at the jumble of arroyos and canyons choked with juniper and piñon pine, and something whacked into the cantle of my saddle. At the same time, I heard the shot, off to my right.

I fell out of the saddle, dragging the carbine

with me, and went flat on my face behind Sox. I was looking out between Sox's legs, toward the sun, and couldn't see a thing on the shadow side of the hill where I thought the shot had come from. I stared till my eyes watered.

After a minute I led Sox to the side of the road and tied him to a tree with the mecate, and moved to the edge of the road where the side dropped away, down into an arroyo. I laid down beside a hump of dirt.

Nothing happened for quite a while. Then I thought I saw something move on that side of the hill two or three hundred yards across the arroyo. Then, again, nothing happened, and I was about to get up, when a rider topped out, showing black against the sky. I shot four times as fast as I could, but I couldn't tell whether I had hit him.

Sox began to buck, and I had to run across and grab the tie rope before he broke loose. By the time I had quieted him down, there was nobody in sight over there.

I dug the slug out of the cantle with my pocket knife. It was battered out of shape, but it looked like a 44.40.

I got on and began to ride up the road, and the farther I went, the madder I got. Nobody had followed me out from town. I hadn't seen a soul except those wagons in Granite Dells, and that jerk line freight rig a mile or so back, until I saw Johnny Moore. Harry Peters or him could have been in town last night, looking for me or not, and would most likely know I had the money on me. Or maybe they didn't know about the money, but either of them could have taken a crack at me just for the hell of it. Or maybe Moyers was sore about the price I'd gouged out of him, and thought he'd trade back for one rifle slug.

I turned Sox around and kicked him into a trot. When I got back to the freight rig, I stopped and asked the skinner if he'd seen anybody, but he hadn't. I had my carbine over my arm, and he said, "You look kind of on the prod."

I showed him the mushroomed 44.40 slug. "I suppose you'd just forget it if somebody tried to cut you down with this?" I asked him.

"My God!" he said. "Where'd you dig that out of?"

"Damn near out of my ass. If the cantle of my saddle hadn't got in the way."

"Prob'ly some kid after antelope. I seen a bunch of them in with some cows back there."

"You figure I look like a pronghorn riding a horse?"

"I thought I heard a shot," he said. He began to swear at his mules, and got a stone out of a sack on his saddlehorn. He threw it and hit his nigh leader on the rump, and the team leaned into their collars.

I rode on and tied Sox back in the brush, a quarter of a mile from the gate where the road went to the cabin. I'd cooled down some. I couldn't prove who shot at me, and I'd have let it go, because if things turned out right I'd be running the Ram House Trading Post pretty soon with Callie, and maybe never go back to Prescott or anywhere where Harry Peters was. Nobody had got my money, either. But if him or Johnny Moore wanted to, they could catch me easy, get ahead of me and have another try at bushwhacking, and I wasn't going to go on riding with my chin hung over my shoulder looking back, or having to worry whether every cutbank or clump of brush had a cocked 44.40 pointing at me.

I knew every inch of that section of land, and I got right up to the cabin without anybody seeing me. Joe Ochoa's horse and another were tied outside. There was a carbine in the boot on Joe's horse, and I went over to it. The horse shuffled around some, but nobody came out of the cabin. Smoke was coming out of the stove pipe, and the door was open, and I heard people talking inside.

I pulled Joe's carbine out and smelled the

muzzle, and eased back the lever and smelled the receiver, but I didn't think it had been shot recently. I walked over to the cabin and leaned on the door frame, looking in. Moyers was talking to Joe. He said, "Burn all the junk, Joe, and clean it up. We'll use the place for tool storage and barbwire."

Joe said, "All right, Mr. Moyers. What about this . . . ?" Then he saw me with my carbine in my hands. His mouth stayed open.

Moyers said, "Better fix the roof, too. Hey, what the hell's wrong with you?" and swung around to see what Joe was staring at.

I said, "Where's Harry and Johnny?"

"Why . . . why. . . ." he kind of spluttered, and said, "what the hell do you want? You told me you wouldn't come back here!"

I tossed the 44.40 slug at him, and he caught it and looked at it.

"Johnny sent me a little going away present. About an hour ago, up the road. Or maybe Harry. Where they at?"

"You're crazy! Harry's in town. You loosened a couple of his teeth for him. He went in to get 'em fixed."

"He never passed me on the road."

Joe Ochoa said, "Yesterday. His teeth hurt him, and he went in yesterday afternoon."

"What caliber's his carbine?"

"44.40," Joe said.

49

"So what about Johnny? Did he get a new carbine?"

"He was goin' to," Joe said. "I don' know if he did."

"Where's he at, now? I wanta talk to him."

"He's shoeing some horses at head-quarters," Moyers said.

"How long you been here?"

"Why, I don't know. Couple of hours, maybe," Moyers said.

"Then you don't know if he's shoeing horses, or maybe he's out in the brush with a new carbine. You fellows go back to work. I'll ride over to the blacksmith shop."

Moyers said, "We'll all go, then. You're not going to start any more trouble, Conway."

And just then Johnny Moore rode up and tied his horse and came in. When he saw me, he began to stutter and his eyes near popped out.

I said, "Let's see your carbine, Johnny."

"I . . . I ain't got one," he said. "Ain't had time to go to town. What the hell's the matter here?"

Well, I couldn't prove anything, and time was wasting.

"Guess I'll ride, Moyers. You keep your two boys home a couple of days. Anybody from here follows me, I'll stretch him out. That goes for you, too. I ain't sure you wouldn't like to see that money back in your pocket. That plain enough?"

"You're insulting, Conway," he said. "And you're a stupid, suspicious fool."

"Sure. You keep that 44.40 slug I'm so suspicious of, for a reminder. I owe somebody one. So send somebody after me if you want."

I walked away. Just before I went around a bend in the road, I looked back, and they were all three standing there watching me go.

I didn't really think anybody would follow me any more, and nothing happened, and I rode into Jerome about ten P.M.

CHAPTER 4

That copper town, spilling down the sides of the ravines and washes on the slope of the mountain, was as noisy and busy by night as by day. The freighters, off-shift miners, and other miscellaneous drunks kept the saloon doors and the roulette wheels in motion, and the dealers worked in shifts at the poker and faro layouts. I had two drinks and a hot dinner, put Sox in a livery barn, and got a hotel room.

I was on my way at sun up, with the

whole Verde Valley spread out north and east below me, and the smelter at Clarkdale pouring yellow smoke into the sky. It was a long haul for Sox after we went through Cottonwood and another twenty miles to the new town of Sedona – at least, the post office was new that year, and there wasn't much else – then up the long, steep trail to the Mogollon Rim, seven thousand feet in the air, where the ponderosa pines took over from the junipers. There was plenty of graze for Sox, and I built a little fire of pine knots and rolled up beside it. I woke up toward morning tied in knots and shivering, and there was frost on my tarp. I huddled over the fire till daylight, and ate jerky and crackers. Half frozen, I rode ten more miles into Flagstaff before noon, had a hot meal, and rode on.

It was another long haul north to Cameron, mostly logging roads through the pines, with the San Francisco peaks just west. There were thousands of acres of aspens like somebody had splattered a huge bucket of yellow paint across the pine forest. Eighteen hours in the saddle ... that tiny, red-rock hotel by the trading post, beside the dry bed of the Little Colorado, looked awful good to me.

Next day, still heading north, I got a coffee pot and a pound of Arbuckle's coffee at the trading post in Tuba City, where the Navajo kids went to school – the ones that didn't manage to hide from the Bureau of Indian Affairs people.

I took the wagon road east, then, splitting off from the road to Lee's Ferry way up on the Colorado River, and went past Moenkopi Wash where the Hopi's had their cornfields, right in the middle of their old enemies, the Navajos. I made another dry camp under Howell Mesa that night, and next day rode past the three Hopi Mesas with the villages with the funny names, like Hotevilla, Oraibi, Shongopovi, Mishongnovi or Walpi. I had to look hard to tell which was houses and which was big chunks of rock way up on the cliffs. Lieutenant Haverhill told me once that a couple of those villages had been lived in for a thousand years.

I had a good meal farther on at Keams Canyon, where the Hopi kids went to school. They were easier to catch than the Navajo kids, because there were only a few steep trails up to their mesas, and the cliffs were straight up and down. Sometimes the missionaries and officials actually dragged them out of their houses, cut their hair, dragged them off to school, and even threatened the parents with guns if they objected. I made the Hubbell Trading Post at Ganado, that night.

I hadn't ever met Don Lorenzo Hubbell

when I went through Ganado on my way to the Ram House Ruin dig, but he welcomed me and gave me dinner in that big dining room with all the paintings, baskets, Navajo rugs, and old prehistoric pots. A lot of famous people had had their dinner there – presidents, congressmen, famous writers. It hit me all the stronger what a wonderful life this was . . . helping the Navajos and making an honest living at the same time, and all that space around you and nobody to bother you.

When he opened up in the morning, there were three wagons waiting with stinking sheepskins to trade, and several families on horseback with the women holding babies in cradleboards on the horns of their homemade saddles. The saddles were decorated with rows of brass tacks and the bridles loaded with silver. Mr. Hubbell talked Navajo as fast as the Navajos did, and there was a lot of laughing and joking. The Navajos must have really liked him to open up like that, because generally they didn't have any use for white men. I guess you wouldn't have lasted very long as a trader, though, if they didn't like you and trust you. It made me all the more anxious to get my hands on the Ram House Trading Post and start living the kind of a life Mr. Hubbell had.

I told him I was going to visit Old Man

Beasley at the Ram House post, and that I had been on the Ram House Ruin dig with Lieutenant Haverhill. He said, "Give the old goat my regards. We get kind of worried about him, with that rheumatism and all, and nobody around. Say, you'll be going past Chinle. Will you take a note to Sam Day, at the post there?"

"Sure," I said. "Be glad to."

He said, "If you never saw Canyon de Chelly, it'd be worth your while to ride along the edge and take a look down. That's about the most beautiful place in the world."

He put me up some sandwiches, and I took the note, thanked him, and rode out.

Going north, up Beautiful Valley – that was its name, and it was sure the truth – between Pine Springs Wash and Bis-E-Ahi Wash, I almost felt like I was coming home after being away a long time. The wind had an edge that would peel your hide, and I buttoned my blanket-lined coat clear to the neck and tied my bandanna over my ears. I felt all warm inside and kind of light, like some big knot had come loose. Big fat white clouds sailed like a flock of sheep in a sky bluer than you could imagine, and the brown grass waved like ripples on a lake, and there was never a fence as far as you could see, and nobody swearing or fighting, no stamp mills hammering or smelter smoke dirtying up the sky. Just the world like God made it with the people and their houses fitting into it and belonging to it like the rocks, junipers, yucca, coyotes, and antelope. You had to look hard to see a hogan, even when the smoke gave it away. Those little houses made of rock, logs or dirt were either six- or eight-sided or round, with domed roofs of dirt. The only opening was a low door, always facing the east. There weren't many, at least within sight of the road. Every one had a corral of crooked, upright sticks tied together with rawhide, and a summer shelter, just a pole frame with cottonwood branches for a roof.

I only passed two wagons in the whole twenty-five miles to Chinle. One, with two water barrels and a load of firewood, was driven by an old man with a red rag around his head. There was a squaw on the seat. I waved and hollered "Good morning," but they didn't hear me or see me, ten feet away. Even their two dogs didn't pay any attention to me.

There was a young squaw driving the next one I saw with a load of sheepskins covered with a ragged tarp. I pulled up and remembered the Navajo for 'Hello' or 'Good Morning', or something like that. I said, *"Yah-ah-tay!"* but she never even turned her head, just drove on past.

There were horses running loose, some of them pretty good, and some awful. It's funny how there's something different about an Indian horse or dog . . . you can't quite put your finger on it, but as soon as you see one something tells you it's Indian.

Then I'd see a flock of sheep, and look all around and not see a hogan anywhere. It was like they just sprouted out of the earth along with the goats and two or three dogs to keep them bunched up and chase in the strays. The herders were women or girls, some of them not over six or seven. They either walked or rode a burro or horse, and were dressed up like they were going to a Squaw Dance – bright colored velvet blouses, skirts almost trailing on the ground. Silver and turquoise jewelry hung around their necks and on their arms under the blankets they wore. And I was still the invisible man. Near or far, they looked right through me.

Well, I thought, you wait! Pretty soon I'll be "Hosteen" Conway to you, or have a Navajo name you'll hang on me. I'll be taking your silver jewelry in pawn, and dickering with you over sheepskins and rugs, and we'll all be friends. Which brought Callie to mind again, because I was going to need her, or somebody that could talk Navajo, or I'd have to learn the language. But with Callie there to do the talking, it would be wonderful! Once your luck breaks it keeps on going, and I knew, way down inside, that everything was going to turn out right. I'd have my trading post and my sweet Callie, and a life that couldn't be better if I sat down and invented it.

I rode through the scatter of hogans that made up Chinle and down to the trading post about two in the afternoon. I gave Hubbell's note to the trader, name of Sam Day. He gave me coffee, and we sat a while. He said the Chinle post was one of the earliest on the reservation, along with the Hubbell's and the Wetherill's over at Kayenta. He was curious about me, but I only said I'd been on that dig at Ram House Ruin, and had quit my job and was just loose-footing it around, and planned to visit Old Man Beasley a few days. He said he couldn't see why anyone wanted to visit Beasley. I told him I wanted to take a look down into Canyon de Chelly, too, and he looked like he thought I was simple in the head. Anyhow, he said to take the dirt road east along the south edge, the road that went on to Fort Defiance.

I followed the road for a mile or so and kept looking to my left, but couldn't see any canyon. Then, all of a sudden it was there. It dropped straight off for maybe eight hundred feet to a flat sand floor a quarter of a mile wide. A stream twisted across the sand, reflecting the sky. It looked like somebody had spilled a pot of melted silver that ran slowly through the canyon. Along the far side at the foot of the cliff, a strip of old cottonwoods, with some leaves still on them, was butter yellow. They were reflected in the creek, too, like gold had melted into the silver. Under them were two hogans with smoke curling out of the smoke holes, and I could just make out a flock of sheep being pushed into a brush corral.

I remembered what Lieutenant Haverhill had told me, that you pronounced de Chelly like "de Shay." That was what the Americans made out of a kind of fake Spanish word, "de Chelly," that they pronounced "de Shay-yee." The Spanish got it from the Navajo word *tsegi* that just meant canyon. He told me about Kit Carson making the Navajos surrender in 1864 and quit raiding the Hopis and other Pueblos along the Rio Grande, and the whites during the Civil War. The Navajos thought they could stand him off down in the canyon. He killed their sheep and horses, burned their cornfields, and chopped down their peach trees. After that they quit, and the government sent them to Bosque

Redondo in New Mexico Territory for a few years. Haverhill told me, too, that back around 1804 a bunch of Navajos hiding in a cave up Canyon del Muerto, which branched off from Canyon de Chelly on the north side, were hiding from Spanish troops. They would have been all right, but one old squaw couldn't keep her mouth shut and yelled some dirty insult. The Spaniards couldn't get them out of the cave, so they shot their muskets against the roof, and the ricochets killed all the Navajos. He said the skeletons were still there.

That was a world all its own down there, like nothing I'd ever seen. I rode a few more miles, looking for another place where I could get a good look down into the canyon. When I found it, there across on the other side, in a cave a little way up from the canyon floor, was a ruin. It must have been pretty big, but it looked real small down there, and the cliff was a sheer wall of rock straight up and down for over a thousand feet. The second story of the ruin was white, plaster of some kind or white rocks, and I knew it was the White House that Haverhill had talked about, maybe a thousand years old. Some day I was going to climb into that ruin and explore it. I looked a long time, and then rode on. It must have been ten miles from Chinle where the road cut south, away from the canyon, and I could look across at Spider Rock. Its top was level with the rim where I was, and was all white from bird droppings – eagles had a nest there, I guess. It was a thin tower, and it stuck right straight up from the canyon floor all by itself. That's where the Spider Woman lived, according to the Navajos. She taught the first Navajo women to weave, and if their kids misbehaved, she would carry them off to her nest and eat them. They told the kids the white stuff was the bones of bad children the Spider Woman had eaten.

I'd been so interested in the canyon I forgot about time, and I knew it was too far to go back to Chinle and then go on to the Ram House Trading post, another thirty or more miles. I decided to ride back to Chinle and ask Mr. Day if I could stay the night with him.

It was dark before I got back, and down to freezing, and for a while I was afraid I was lost. But Sox followed the wagon track easy enough, and after a while I saw sparks spiraling up from the smoke holes of some hogans, and then a light in the back of the trading post.

Mr. Day wasn't too glad to see me, but he gave me some cold roast mutton and some stale, store-bought bread that I guess was brought all the way from Gallup by wagon.

He showed me to a small bedroom and I went to see if Sox was all right in the corral. When I came back in, Mr. Day locked up again and went to bed.

I peeled down to my socks and long johns and climbed into bed. It was a half hour before I could straighten out my legs, that bed was so cold. And next thing I knew, it was morning, and I smelled coffee and heard pots rattling. My feet near froze on the packed dirt floor before I could stamp into my boots, and I had to break the ice in the pitcher before I could fill the wash basin. I sure wasn't going to shave with ice water, and as it happened, I never did shave again for almost four months.

When I went into the kitchen, Sam Day's helper was there having breakfast with him, a tall, young Navajo named Bi-zah-dee. I found out later that meant "the talker" or "the gabber," but he didn't say anything at all when Mr. Day introduced us, even though he talked some English. He just looked through me like I wasn't there.

I had my breakfast – bacon, fried potatoes, and coffee – said thanks to Mr. Day, and went out to the corral. Sox and a couple of other horses were blowing steam and working on the hay someone had tossed down for them. I gave him time to finish, then saddled up and was about to lead him out and walk him in a few circles, when a wagon drove up to the post.

A real good looking young Navajo woman got down, took a quick look at me, didn't see me at all – for all the sign she made – and went inside. When I was on that Ram House Ruin dig with Lieutenant Haverhill, I saw a lot of Navajo girls and women, families of the Navajos that worked for us ... but never anything like this one! I took a turn around the hitchrail with Sox's reins and went inside. I was sure I was out of Bull Durham, or something else I really needed.

The girl, Bi-zah-dee, and Mr. Day were going into the kitchen, and Day turned to me with a knowing grin on his face and said, "You must've forgot something, hey? Well, come on and have another cup of coffee."

I grinned and stuck out my hand, and said, "Link Conway, Miss ..." but the girl didn't see it, or me either. Just went on and sat at the kitchen table. Day and I sat down, too, and Bi-zah-dee poured each of us a cup of coffee and sat down.

The girl, Mary Wilson, began to talk Navajo real fast with Sam Day, and Day and Bi-zah-dee were laughing and talking back to her, and all acting like I didn't exist. I had a real good look at her. She sure was pretty! Well, maybe pretty isn't the word. I guess you'd say handsome, if you can use that word for a woman. Her face wasn't real dark, like some of them, and had a good strong nose and curved mouth, and real black eyes and eyebrows. She had hung her Pendleton blanket on the back of her chair, and her clothes and jewelry were beautiful – her blouse light blue velveteen with dimes and quarters around the neck and down the sleeves, and her long outer skirt sort of burnt-orange sateen. She wore two heavy, sand-cast bracelets on each wrist, turquoise and silver rings on both hands, and a great big squash-blossom necklace set with turquoise. Her hair was as black as obsidian and just as shiny, and there was a lot of it, clubbed behind her head in that figure-eight knot they called the *chongo*, wrapped with turn after turn of soft, white yarn. The more I looked, the more I could see she was not just pretty or handsome, she was downright beautiful.

Well, I sort of came to, and realized they had stopped talking, and Sam Day and the helper were grinning at me, and the girl was looking at me for the first time, kind of haughty and half mad. I hadn't realized how hard I was staring at her.

Sam Day said, "You look kind of dazed, Conway, like somebody whacked you with a club."

I said, "I didn't mean to be rude, but man,

ain't she something! Sure fills that shirt, don't she! If she took a real deep breath, I think it'd bust open!"

Well, I never was so embarrassed – and not only on account of what I said, but what she said – because like a damn fool I'd taken it for granted she didn't talk English.

She sort of spit it out, "You son of a bitch white-eyes! You got eyes like a pair of hands. I could feel them all over me like I didn't have any clothes on!"

Bi-zah-dee had quit smiling, but Sam Day was grinning like a Chessy cat. I said, "Aw, look, Sister! I didn't mean anything wrong!"

"Don't call me Sister! I couldn't be your sister . . . I'm legitimate!"

First, I was mad at her calling me a bastard that way, and then it struck me funny, and I began to laugh. Day guffawed and slapped his leg, and she began to grin. Only Bi-zah-dee wasn't laughing. I guess he didn't know what legitimate meant. I said, "Look, I apologize! I didn't mean anything raw, I just meant . . ."

"Go on, meant what?"

"I meant I never saw a woman as good looking as you, if you must know! And I don't figure that's anything to get sore about!"

Well, it was her turn to be embarrassed, and her face got darker, and she turned away and put her hand over her mouth the way they

65

all do when they're bashful or embarrassed.

Sam Day said, "Cut it out, you two. Be friends. Conway, this is Mary Wilson. I'd call her a friend of mine, only she won't trade with me. Always does her trading at Ram House Post with Old Man Beasley." But I could tell the way he said it and smiled at her, he thought she was pretty fine.

"That where you're heading?" he asked her.

"Aw, you know why, Sam. He's been awful good to me since . . ." She didn't finish that, but went on, "I've got half a dozen sheep skins. Not enough for you to bother with, anyway. And I've got to start laying in winter supplies."

Day said, "Conway, here, is going to Ram House Post, too. Maybe you'll ride along together."

She looked me in the eye, and she wasn't smiling, now. "I haven't got room for any passengers."

"Why, I wouldn't bother you for anything. You won't catch Link Conway slugging along a mile an hour in some busted down wagon, not while I've got a horse to carry me!"

"If you didn't, I still haven't got room," she said. "Well, I'll be going, Sam. See you tomorrow, on my way home."

She got up and took her blanket off the chair, and I said, "Thanks for the coffee and

66

the hospitality, Mr. Day. I'll hurry and get out of Miss Wilson's way, so she can have the road all to herself!"

I hurried out, and got behind Sox, where he stood at the hitchrack, and jerked a long hair out of his tail. Mary Wilson hadn't come out, yet. I took two turns around Sox's off hind pastern with the horsehair, and tied it tight. It couldn't do him any harm, but it would feel different and uncomfortable to him. I unwrapped his reins and led him a few steps, and he favored his off hind foot, and limped like he had a stone bruise or something. I led him over and leaned against Mary Wilson's wagon, just before she came out.

She said, "Well! I thought you'd be half way to Ram House Post! What's the matter? Don't know which end of your horse you should point that way? Or can't you figure which foot should go in the nigh stirrup so you'll be facing front when you get on?"

"All right! So I shot off my mouth! Now my horse is lame, and I've gotta crawl on my face and ask you if I can tie him onto your tailgate and ride with you."

"I'm pretty good with horses. Let me have a look." But I started to walk away and led Sox after me and he limped like he had a bowed tendon.

"All right," she said, climbed over the

wheel, got on the seat and wrapped the blanket around herself. I tied Sox to the tailgate with the tie rope, and climbed up on the near side of the seat.

She whacked her off horse with the ends of the reins, and we started off at a trot. She had a good team, a lot better than the poor wrecks most Navajos drove, and the harness was clean and oiled, and all of it there except the breeching, which Navajos didn't use much. Her wagon was a good one, too, heavier built than the ones the Studebaker company and some others made special for the Indian trade. Old Sox didn't have any trouble keeping up, and I figured that horsehair would break or come loose before long and he'd quit limping ... I just hoped my driver wouldn't turn around and notice when that happened.

Then for quite a while she wouldn't talk, wouldn't answer anything I asked her, and wouldn't look at me. But at last she said, "You're like every other Goddamn white-eyes. You think because you're white, you can say any dirty thing you want to to an Indian girl, or try things that would get you shot if she was white ... and she'll be so flattered, she'll faint from pure happiness, and fall right on her back. Only before she passes out, she'll just have time to pull her skirt up and spread her legs."

I got mad then. I said, "Listen! I didn't mean anything bad by what I said back there. Actually, it was a compliment, and no different than I'd say about some good looking white girl. Only it happens I meant it, when I said you're the best looking woman I ever saw. And I haven't tried any rough stuff on you, and I haven't got any plans to. And I just noticed my horse is all right now. So haul up, and I'll be glad to get off. Thanks for the ride."

She smiled at me, then, and said, "Let's forget it. I haven't met many white gentlemen, yet, but I'll consider you one till you prove different. Say, show me that trick you did with your horse's foot, will you? Maybe I'll find it handy sometime."

We both laughed, then, and I told her about the horsehair, and after that, it was a pleasant ride. She didn't just start gabbling about herself, and she never asked a single question about me, but she did answer some of the things I asked her. Others, she wouldn't say a word. Naturally, I wondered how she'd learned to speak such good English. Well, she'd finished grade school like a lot of other Navajo kids, at Tuba City. But her father wanted her to have a good education, and sent her to the Sherman Institute of Riverside, California, an all-Indian school

69

run by the government that had students from a lot of tribes, not only Navajos and Hopis. That was pretty unusual for a Navajo father. Most of them didn't want their kids to go even to grammar school, and a lot of them built hogans in places so hard to get to that the authorities never did find them. But Mary Wilson wouldn't tell me a thing about her father and mother, just shut up and acted as if I hadn't asked. She wouldn't tell me where she lived, either, or what she did for a living. I got the idea her folks were dead, though she didn't say so outright. She had only a half dozen or so raw sheepskins to trade, where if she had a big sheep herd, like most of them, she'd have a whole wagon load. On the other hand, she said she had a long list of supplies she had to get for winter, and a half dozen sheepskins wouldn't begin to pay for that list.

The sky was clouded over. It must have been down to freezing, and before we got to the Ram House Trading Post it began to snow. We rode the last mile behind a wagon, with the old man in his flat-brim, black hat and old, worn-out Levi's paying us no mind. His fat wife in a green and red striped Pendleton blanket, a purple satin skirt, and high moccasins sat beside him staring straight ahead. Three little girls and a boy were grinning and gabbling, and turning their faces away whenever I caught their eye. There were two empty water barrels in the wagon.

There was a half inch of snow, and the long, low, main building was dark gray against the white. It was built out of rock, the courses laid up almost as neat as cut stone, but they were natural. You could find any shape and size of building stone lying around. The mullioned windows were small glass panes, all with bars like a jail. The roof was flat, held up by thick pine *vigas*. Smoke was pouring out of the stove pipe sticking through the roof.

Over behind the trading building was a big corral with a good, heavy wagon beside it, and down in a hollow, an iced-over tank made by an earth dam across a wash. The road went on past the tank, just a rough track that went another fifteen miles to the Ram House Ruin, where I worked on the dig those two summers. In a row alongside a big warehouse back of the trading post were three neat guest hogans, for Navajos that might come fifty miles to trade.

There were a dozen Navajos in front of the post, not counting the kids. A couple of the young men had their hair cut – probably they'd been to school – but all the rest were long-hairs. The men all wore silver and turquoise jewelry, even old bow-guards

71

on their left wrist, which weren't of use any more except for decoration. They were all drinking red soda pop, or maybe tomatoes right out of the can. Some of the young men yelled at Mary Wilson, and she hollered back; but I was surprised that none of the older ones said a word to her, or even looked at us. I thought maybe it was because she had a white man with her.

A quarter mile away was the board-and-batten building with its roof falling in, the mission that Callie's father started. I couldn't read the old sign from where I was, but I'd seen it before – "Evangelical Mission. JESUS LIVES!" Past the mission a ways was a good stone cabin that nobody lived in. I found out later that Mary Wilson was born and raised there.

Even when they were fat, the women looked handsome because of the clothes they wore. Some of the young ones were downright pretty. Their hair black and shiny, done up in a *chongo* knot, their blouses every color you could think of, made of velveteen with dimes and quarters sewed around the collars and down the sleeves, and maybe three necklaces of turquoise nuggets or the squash-blossom design, and four or five heavy sandcast bracelets, with turquoise stones. They weave beautiful rugs and blankets, and I don't know why they all buy Pendleton blankets woven way over in Oregon. They all wore four or five skirts made out of bright colored satin, or maybe printed cotton.

Just as we drove up, two young women untied their horses from the hitchrack in front of the store and flipped their four or five skirts up, and swung up into the saddles, sitting astride. They were so clever at it, you only caught a little flash of a brown leg, and the skirt settled neat as can be over the cantle without getting all bunched up. But what tickled me . . . they didn't bother to brush off the half inch of snow on those saddles. The young bucks were all laughing, and the two girls hollered some insult back, and went racing off across the sage flats.

I got down from the wagon and tied Sox at the hitchrack. Old Man Beasley was standing in the door of the post just exactly like he was two years ago, his scraggly old hair done up Navajo-style in the *chongo* knot behind his neck, whiskers down to his chest, thin hook nose sticking out of them under little, watery, blue eyes, and the eyebrows that looked like two tufts of cotton. He had on a greasy, worn, tweed coat and flannel shirt, bib overalls, and Navajo moccasins that came up around his ankles, where the rawhide thong fastened with a silver concha. I never knew why they

73

called them "squaw boots", because both men and women wore them.

He didn't smile or offer to shake hands or anything. He just looked sour, like always, and said, "What's so all-fired funny?"

I said, "Hello, Mr. Beasley! Why, those two girls. They didn't even wipe the snow off their saddles. I bet their underpants are soaking wet!"

"Their ass. They wear all them skirts and no underpants. Sittin' bare-ass on a saddle covered with snow don't make no sense to you and me, but don't start tryin' to figure what makes sense to an Indian. Most times they'll make better sense than you."

I started to ask him if he remembered me, but he walked past me like I wasn't there, and said, "Hello, Adezhbah! Where you been keepin' yourself?"

"Yah-ah-tay, Hosteen Sahni!" Mary said. She had climbed down from the wagon, and she was smiling. She put her arm around his shoulders. "I thought I better come and see if you got another sweetheart while I've been gone!"

"Hell," he said. "You're more'n I can handle, all by yourself." He was actually grinning at her. "Come on in. Coffee's hot, an' I'll rustle up some supper for you."

"I'll put the team up first."

74

"Go on in," I told her. "I'll put your team in the corral."

"All right," she said, but she didn't smile or say thank you. She climbed into the wagon and handed the few sheepskins down to Old Man Beasley, and they went into the trading post.

The Navajos outside were starting to leave. I pulled the saddle, saddlebags and bed roll off Sox and put them inside the door. Then, I drove the wagon down to the corral and turned the team and Sox inside.

I still wasn't sure Old Man Beasley remembered me, but when I went into the post, he hollered from the kitchen to bolt the door and come in and eat. The kitchen was warm and comfortable with the fire in the big black stove, and two kerosene lamps in the brackets on the wall.

I sat at the table, and Mary Wilson set a place for herself and me and served canned corn beef, hot, canned tomatoes, and lumpy biscuits I guess the old man had made. He had coffee with us. He and Mary talked Navajo and didn't pay any attention to me. I knew she was staying over, because it was too dark to leave, and anyway, her team was in the corral. I wondered where we were all going to sleep, and maybe whether Beasley wasn't going to invite me to stay.

75

When we were through eating, the old man sat picking his teeth, then turned to me and said, "What you want here, Conway?" He remembered me, all right.

"Well, when I was up here on that dig, I never had time to look around, and I kind of liked it. So I thought I'd ride around a little and see some things I missed. You got a place I can sleep?"

"You ain't on the dodge?"

"No. I saved up a little money and quit my job. I'm not gonna freeze to death riding fence this winter. You got a room for me?"

"It'll cost you."

Mary got up and stacked the plates in the sink. She said, "Anybody in the hogans?" and I remembered the three guest hogans Beasley had for Navajos from far away.

Beasley said, "The little one's best, Mary. I never let anyone else use that one. There's firewood and water, and you can take the blankets from the middle bedroom."

She went into the hall in back of the kitchen, and came out with an armful of Pendleton blankets. She said, "Good night, Pop, see you in the morning," never said a word to me, and went out. Beasley followed her into the store room and bolted the door, and came back to the kitchen.

He took one of the lamps and showed me

through a hall that led off the kitchen to three small bedrooms, and told me to put my gear in the end one. He set the lamp on an old dresser that had a big bowl and a pitcher of water on it. There was one chair, and a big, sway-backed, double bed, and in the far corner was a pole with a curtain hung from it, and a few big nails in the wall to hang your clothes on. There was one small window with bars on the outside, and the walls were part adobe bricks and part laid-up rock masonry.

After I brought my gear in, I went back to the kitchen, and Beasley said, "How long you gonna be here?"

"I don't know. A few days. What's this costing me?"

"Two dollars a day, for you and your horse."

"No," I told him. "That's too much."

"Can you cook at all?" he wanted to know.

"Why, sure. Biscuits and fried potatoes and meat, things like that."

"A dollar a day, and you cook," he said, and he stumped down the hall, went into the first bedroom, and shut the door.

Well, like in Sam Day's post the night before, I damn near froze before I got the bed warmed up. While I thawed it out, I got to thinking about Callie, and I felt a little guilty, because that Navajo girl, Mary

Wilson – Adezhbah, Beasley had called her – had kind of crowded Callie out of my mind all day long. But what the hell! She was nothing but a real good looking squaw that any man couldn't help looking at, but that didn't mean I didn't love Callie.

Well, I slept like somebody had sandbagged me, and didn't wake up till broad daylight. Old Man Beasley had left the coffee on the back of the stove, and a slab of bacon and some bread on the table. I looked out into the store room, the "bull pen" they called it, and he was behind the counter. There were half a dozen Navajos standing around like they were petrified, not moving and saying nothing.

I asked Beasley where Mary Wilson was, and he said she'd harnessed up, loaded on supplies, and left an hour ago.

I went in and had my breakfast, then went down to the corral and fed Sox, and Beasley's team – a real good matched pair of Morgans – then walked back up the hill to the post.

CHAPTER 5

If you never saw a trading post, it might interest you. There was stuff stacked in the corners and hanging from the *vigas* and from nails in the wall – harness, rope, lanterns, buckets, hardware, horseshoes, crosscut saws, axes, traps. And on the shelves, bolts of Riverside cotton plaid, cotton, velveteen, sateen, double LL sheeting. Levi pants and jackets, work shirts, Stetson and Mallory hats, work shoes, saddle and collar pads. Overhead were saddles, bridles with bits, and coils of rope.

Stacked on the floor against the wall near a three-foot high pile of Navajo rugs were sacks of flour and sugar, crates of paper sacks of Arbuckle's coffee, small sacks of table salt, cases of Lytona baking powder, cans of tomatoes and peaches, and barrels of crackers. There were slabs of chewing tobacco, cartons of Bull Durham cigarette tobacco, and much, much more. And everything under a layer of sand and dust. In the adjoining warehouse were tons of sheepskins and pelts, and piñon nuts in sacks, taken in trade.

About the most interesting thing in the

store was the separate room where the pawned jewelry was kept. It opened off the main room, and fastened with a padlock. Every piece had its own pawn tag – the belts with embossed silver conchas five inches in diameter, studded with turquoise, coral, and sea shell; the silver and turquoise bow guards; the rings, bracelets, earrings, and hair ornaments; the heavy squash-blossom design necklaces, and the necklaces of lumps of turquoise and coral. Sometimes Beasley lent them back to their owners for special occasions, like a Sing or a Squaw Dance. They were not for sale, until put in dead pawn after three years. Then the trader could sell them.

I stood around most of the afternoon, mostly behind the counter watching Old Man Beasley measure out cloth, sugar, and flour, check his credit clips and charge items. Some of the Navajos were taller than me, but from behind the counter they looked shorter, and that had me puzzled. Beasley told me the floor behind the counter was four inches higher than out in the bull pen. It sort of gave the trader the advantage, made him look bigger, and the Navajos had to look up to him. He said all the traders had them like that.

There was a small wooden box with Bull Durham and papers nailed to the counter, and the bucks would come up and roll a free cigarette. The women would take an hour to decide between ten yards of red rickrack braid and ten yards of green. The men would go off into dreamland studying the price of thirty feet of rope, and then maybe not buy it. The kids always managed to wheedle hard candy and strawberry pop from the old folks.

The women sat on a bench along the wall on the right side of the room because, Old Man Beasley said, that's the woman's side of the hogan.

There was one bit of excitement to break up the slow business, the low voices, and the drawn out haggling. That was when someone made a remark to a young buck rolling a cigarette at the free box. A fat old girl was waddling in the door, and he dropped the cigarette and hurried out, keeping his back to the old lady. There was a lot of laughing and jokes, and Beasley told me the old squaw was the young man's mother-in-law, and if he saw her face, he'd go crazy. Beasley said it caused an awful lot of annoyance and trouble, but they all believed it. Some young bucks married their wives' mothers just to get around it. If any Navajo buck ever saw a woman naked, maybe bathing in a tank or coming out of a sweat bath, it would blind him. So maybe they couldn't keep from looking, but they'd put a hand over one eye, so as to salvage at least that much.

Beasley said he was going to close up and I could get supper, so I started to go into the big kitchen in back. He stopped me, "Wash your hands real good. Don't put them to your face or eyes until you've washed. A lot of these people have trachoma, that's a disease that makes them blind, and it's catching. You be careful all the time you're here."

I built up the fire in the big range, washed in hot water, and then peeled potatoes and opened a couple of cans of corned beef. I made biscuits, too, and when the old man came in from closing the store and saw the biscuits, he grinned for the first time. He went and got a can of plum jam.

After dinner, we sat there picking our teeth. I rolled a smoke, tipped back in my chair, and said, "Well, Mr. Beasley, I like it. How much you want for it, cash?"

He picked his teeth a while longer, and finally said, "What is it you like?"

"Why, the place here! The trading post!"

He just sat there looking at me.

"What's the matter? You changed your mind about selling it, have you?"

"Don't recall ever makin' up my mind to sell," he said. "Where'd you git such a notion?"

"Why," I said, "Callie . . . Callie . . ." And

I realized I didn't know her last name.

"Callie! You wouldn't mean Callie Allison, would you?" and I remembered she said her father was named Allison.

"Yeah, that's it. She grew up here. Her father was one of those hell-fire preachers."

"You can't tell me anything about Callie I don't know, exceptin' maybe what devilment she's got into since I saw her last, seven years ago. Where'd you know her?"

"She's working down in Prescott, in the Palace Bar."

"In a saloon? I never thought she'd get that low!"

That got me sore. "She's a decent woman making a decent living. She's a singer, and not anything else!"

"Cool down! I watched her grow up. Some people said she got to be a liar and couldn't be trusted, and the Navvie girls said she put on airs because she was white, an' that she wasn't no better'n she should be around the Navvie boys. Well, maybe they were right an' maybe they were wrong, but I always felt sorry for her, because it was her old man drove her to it with his dirty, suspicious mind. I couldn't really blame her. He was awful quick to use that razor strap on her, for nothin' at all, a lot of times. An' she got so she knew he wouldn't believe the truth. Guess she figured she might

83

as well have the game as the name. She wasn't a bad girl, not deep down inside, she wasn't. No wonder she run off with that no good son of a bitch and never come back, that time she went with the old man to that revival meetin' down to Phoenix."

"What no good son of a bitch?" I asked him, but he didn't answer that.

"So she said I wanted to sell out? An' you believed her? Listen, son, Callie got so she'd lie sometimes even when the truth would serve her better. Got to be a habit, I guess, to protect herself from her father, always accusin' her of everything that came into his dirty mind. But well . . . I have been thinkin' about sellin' out. The old rheumatiz just about kills me winters, an' I get to seein' visions of Santa Barb'ry or Long Beach. You're the first I ever mentioned it to, though. Maybe she's been readin' my mind from a distance, 'cause that's the only way she'd know it. What bothers me is if she told you that, what's *she* figure on gettin' out of it? You tell me that!"

Well, believe me, that had me puzzled. I couldn't believe the old man was lying to me – what reason would he have? But I knew Callie wouldn't lie to me, either. Maybe he just forgot he'd ever said anything to her about selling . . . but then, it sure didn't seem like he'd had it in mind before she left, seven years ago.

Well, it didn't make any difference, so long as he had a mind to sell out, now. And one thing! I thought I knew what was in it for Callie! She was going to marry me, and live with me up here on the reservation. That's why she was so interested. That had to be it!

So I quit worrying about that puzzle and did up the dishes and went to bed. The bed was like ice, but I warmed up under about fourteen pounds of Pendleton blankets.

CHAPTER 6

The floor of my bedroom, like at Chinle, was just packed earth, and I near froze my feet again, in the morning before I got my boots on. I'd heard the old man get up a couple of times in the night and stoke the kitchen fire, so the big kitchen-living room was warm enough. I made another batch of soda biscuits and got breakfast – bacon, coffee, and oatmeal with canned milk.

Beasley was really stove up with rheumatism when he came to the table. He ate like a wolf, though, and leaned back with his second cup of coffee, and said, "An old man gets pretty lonesome around here with nothin' but Navvies to talk to, an' them with nothin' to talk about ... so when somebody comes along, I guess I get to runnin' off at the mouth. Now, what I said about Callie Allison last night ... well, she was the sweetest little girl you ever saw, up to the time her ma couldn't stand that dirty-minded, hell-fire-preachin' bastard anymore, an' ran off. He took it out on Callie, an' when she got big enough so's he couldn't take a strap to her no more, she done a lot of wild, foolish things just to spite him. Drove him near crazy. Made people not like her. But me, I knew why, an' I wouldn't ever turn against her, nor blame her for what she did sometimes. Well, never mind all that."

He poured another cup of coffee, put in too much sugar, and went on, "Now, about me sellin' out, you couldn't buy me out if you wanted to. You were just workin' for wages on that dig two years ago, an' you said you just been cowboyin' since. You got any idea what this place is worth?"

"You tell me. If I really want it, that is. I'm not sure it's what I really want to do with my money."

"I don't own it, not the buildings. Just the stock an' the license from the Bureau. How would you know how to get a license? No experience. No friends in the United States Department of the Interior, an' you don't speak the language."

"Well, what experience did you have when you started? How much Navajo did you talk?"

"I got me a couple of Navajo helpers, man and wife. She done the cookin' an' housekeepin', if you could call it that."

"Well, what's to stop me, then?"

"Mostly, I ain't sure I wanta sell, and you ain't got enough money. I'd have to take inventory, but my stock's worth seven, eight thousand."

"If you're not selling," I said, "that's one thing. But if it's the money, let's talk. Maybe you'd stay around a while and help me get started."

"Well, maybe a few weeks, but winter's comin' on. You never put in no winter up here. You don't know what it's like. First real snow, I'd get out. Go lay on the beach in the sunshine, over in Santa Barb'ry."

"If you'll give me a hand getting the license, maybe put in a good word in the right place, I'll give you five thousand dollars for the place."

"What do you mean? Down payment and fifty a month or something?"

"No, cash money."

"How soon could you get your hands on it?"

"Just as soon as you say the word."

"I'd take sixty-five hundred if you had it."

He wouldn't talk any more, but got up and opened the store. There was a Navajo and his squaw waiting outside, with a pack horse and two sacks of wool to trade. The sacks were made out of Pendleton blankets sewed together and slung over the pack horse. I helped the old man to weigh it, and check to see if it had been wet down or had any stones in it to make it heavier, and he showed me how he set down the credit for their account on a paper sack stuck on a nail in the wall – so much credit for Mr. and Mrs. Harrison Natai. Some other Navajos came in, and Mrs. Natai spent most of two hours picking out a few yards of bright orange sateen. Harrison Natai bought four pounds of hard candy, a slab of plug tobacco, and a pair of Levi's way too long for his bowed old legs. He put them on over what he was wearing and turned the cuffs up six inches. Old Man Beasley waited on some of the others, then subtracted what the Natais bought from their credit. For some reason, Harrison Natai wanted to pay cash for the candy. Beasley mumbled to himself, "Let's see. A quarter pound, that's one yellow. That's four yellows or two blues to the pound. Four pounds is sixteen yellows or eight blues." He said something in Navajo, and Harrison Natai dug eight dimes out of his pocket.

I asked, "What's a yellow?"

"That's a nickel," Beasley answered, "A dime's a blue. Penny's a red. And now you know it, you still don't know how to say it in Navajo, so what good's it do you? There's a hell of a lot more. How come you think you could handle a trading post, even was you to buy one?"

He broke off and said something to a young Navajo rolling a cigarette at the free Bull Durham box, and the Navajo dumped the tobacco back into the box and walked away.

"You gotta watch 'em every minute," Beasley said. "He had two already, since he come in. They'll steal you blind if you give 'em the chance, an' they'll cheat each other playin' poker an' three-card monte, an' get real hoomiliated if they git caught. It ain't the stealin' or cheatin' that anybody minds. They think a man's pretty smart that gits away with it, but he's stupid if he gits caught."

"He's taking a can of tomatoes off the shelf."

"Who?" Beasley asked, and I pointed at the young Navajo.

Beasley grabbed my arm and jerked it down. "Don't ever do that! Don't point at nobody! Scares the hell out of 'em, 'cause it points 'em out to the witches an' devils. Don't ask nobody their name, either. An' don't never call a Navvie a coyote. They got no swear words, but that's worse than anything you could name a man in English. I've seen a man get a knife in the guts for that."

He marked down the can of tomatoes on the young Navajo's account.

I hung around the bull pen all day, asking questions, watching the bargaining, and noticing the way Old Man Beasley sure kept the upper hand and watched everybody like a hawk. He never got mad and never yelled at anybody, and was real polite to the old people. He cracked jokes with the old squaws, and I could tell by the way everybody laughed that they were dirty jokes, but the old girls didn't get mad, either. The Navajos that hung around all day got a little used to me, but the newcomers wouldn't look at me or smile, or answer when I said, "Yah-ah-tay!"

After we locked up and had supper, we sat at the table, me smoking and him chewing and getting up to spit in the stove. I said,

"I don't know if sixty-five hundred is a fair price or not. All I know is I couldn't pay that much. So if you can wait around for three or four more winters, why maybe somebody will come along with a pocketful of money that can't stand to live without owning the Ram House Trading Post."

"I never said I'd sell, and I sure ain't gonna give it away! I might come down a little, but I'd have to have the cash. An' you ain't got it, so this is just a lot of jaw-flappin'. Don't mean a thing."

I shoved back my chair and stood up. "I'll get it. I'll put it right in your hand."

I was going to wave five thousand dollars right under his nose, and go to fifty-five hundred if I had to.

"Don't push at me! I ain't made up my mind. An' even if you got it, I don't wanta see it. Don't tell me where you got it hid. You lose it, or some Navvie steals it, an' I git the blame."

I figured he was afraid to look at it, for fear he wouldn't be able to stand it. I thought I'd let him stew a while, and I went to bed. Before I undressed, I checked on the money. I had pulled a big loose adobe brick out of the wall behind the head of the bed, dug out some mud plaster to make room for it, put the money belt in there, and shoved the brick back flush with the wall. It was still there, all right.

It went that way for three more days, with me helping out in the bull pen and doing the cooking, and helping him count the wool sacks in the warehouse. They weighed three hundred and fifty pounds apiece, and he must've had twenty tons, and eight or ten tons of piñon nuts. I asked him a lot of questions about the business, and he seemed to be trying to teach me all he could, but he didn't say anything more about selling out.

That afternoon there weren't any customers, and the old man and I sat in the kitchen drinking coffee. I said, "I've seen a lot of Navajos, now – big ones, little ones, old ones, young ones, fat, lean, smart, stupid – and I still can't figure Mary Wilson out. She doesn't fit in."

"You're just damn right she don't!"

"The rest of them don't seem to like her very much."

"They don't understand her, an' they're jealous. An' it ain't just 'cause she's half white. They don't give a damn about that."

"Half white! Why, she sure don't look . . ."

"No, she don't. An' she don't know whether she wants to be white or Navajo, an' it's awful hard on her. I've knowed her since she was born, like Callie. Her father never should've sent her to school, not to that Sherman Institute, anyway. That's what made all the trouble. 'Cause she hadn't ever found out before what white people do to Indians. She learned how to cook an' keep house, an' how to typewrite, an' write that shorthand, an' a lot of other things. So then when she graduated nobody would hire her, not no white man, except maybe for a maid. All they wanted was to get her on her back. She came home, then. Now she don't trust anybody but me an' maybe Sam Day, an' part of it's 'cause we're too old to try an' get under her skirts, I guess."

I rolled a smoke and filled my cup. "Well, is she happy now?"

"Damn if I know. The Navvies don't accept her, neither. She tried to help some of the girls when she got back, you know, cookin', an' housekeepin', an' keepin' themselves clean, an' it just made 'em sore. Said she thought she was better 'n them . . . an' I guess she does, an' why shouldn't she? But she oughtn't to let 'em see it. So, anyway, now she's gone Navajo all the way, an' her clothes, an' her wagon, an' her hogan are better 'n any of them. Only she hasn't got a friend in the world but me and Sam Day. We sort of look out for her."

"Well, how does she live? Does she weave

rugs? She couldn't make a living on that alone, could she? Or running a few sheep?"

"Why, her father left her plenty. I mean, she ain't rich, but she ain't ever gonna starve, neither. Come in here, lemme show you."

We went into his bedroom, and there on the wall was a painting of him – of Old Man Beasley – signed with a flourish, "Ellsworth Wilson". It was younger by ten years, but it was him to a T. I'd seen paintings by Charlie Russell and prints of some of Frederic Remington's pictures, but I never knew a man could take a brush, some paint, and make a picture that you'd swear was breathing and was about to talk to you.

"He was a famous artist. He came out from New York to paint pictures for the Santa Fe Railway. They were in magazines, and made into posters to put in advertisements, in the railway stations, an' ticket offices. Seemed like he should've been born on the reservation, he liked it so much. He never did go back east."

Some customers came in then, and we were both busy till closing time. While we were eating supper, I got him started on Mary Wilson again. I said, "What happened to Mary Wilson's folks?"

"Well, he should've known better! They were comin' back from Ganado, an' it was bad weather, thunderstorms all around. He tried to cross Sheepdip Wash, an' they got caught in a flash flood. Maybe he tried to save the team, or maybe she got washed off an' he tried to get her. Anyway, we found the wagon and the team a hundred yards from the crossin', an' them a half mile farther down. That was right after Mary came home from tryin' to make a livin' in Tucson."

"Must've been awful for her!"

"It was pure hell. Listen! I liked them two ... an' I don't wanta talk about it no more."

Then that night, after dinner, he said, "Sixty-five hundred, that strike you right? I'm giving away fifteen hundred dollars' worth of stock, but if I die up here of the rheumatism or the pneumonia, it ain't gonna do me much good."

"Five thousand, cash money. And I'll put it in your hand in two minutes."

"Five thousand? *Hohonya!*" and went limping off to bed. I didn't find out for a long time that *hohonya* means bull shit in Navajo.

Next morning, I said, "Well, I might as well split the breeze. How much I owe you?"

"What's your hurry?" he said, and I took it to mean he didn't want me to go and was still interested in selling.

He began going through the Navajos' accounts with me, showing me the figures on those brown paper sacks, which column was credit, and what was owing on what they bought. He told me about the pawn system and how he loaned on value. Most of the Navajos didn't want to pawn the jewelry for full value, but just a few dollars for something they wanted. Some of the stuff was in and out every two or three weeks. Some of it was pawned for credit for groceries, soda pop, and candy, and some of it had been gathering dust for ten years. Some of it, too, was dead pawn, and the old man had, little by little, loaned more than it was worth. He had a right to sell it. But he said he never did, unless a piece of dead pawn belonged to someone that died, so there was no chance he'd ever get his money back. Tourists came by every once in a while, or maybe geologists or archaeologists that would have paid him a lot for some of it.

He unlocked the pawn room and went in. "There's more 'n twelve thousand dollars worth in here," he said. "O' course, I got no claim in the full value, just what I loan on it. Look here."

He took down a belt from about fifty of them hanging on nails. It had seven five-inch conchas on it and a beautiful sand-cast buckle, and each concha had a big lump of dark blue turquoise in the middle.

"This here gem's turquoise. Best there is, and gettin' scarce. This belt's worth a thousand dollars. And look at this."

He opened a drawer and pulled out a heavy necklace, little silver beads shaped like fancy hollow bells, and between them lumps of dark turquoise with black lines on it like spider webs.

"Squash-blossom necklace," he said. "Only those are really pomegranate blossoms. They copied it from old Spanish silver work. That's matrix turquoise on the big blossom on the end, only that ain't really a blossom. It's what them museum people call a fertility symbol. S'posed to be a woman's womb. This'n's worth more'n the belt."

We heard a wagon pull up outside, and he locked the pawn room and went to the door. He looked out and said, "It's Franklin Yazzie, works for me. Been to Gallup for supplies. Go help him unload, will you?"

Franklin Yazzie was real friendly with me, like one white man to another. He was young, had his hair cut, and wore all white man's clothes ... only his hat was black with a five-inch brim and a high crown without any creases or dents, and had a beaded hat band with an eagle feather stuck in it.

I helped him unload the flour, crates of Arbuckle's and canned tomatoes and such, and asked him how he learned to speak English like that. He said he'd been to school at Tuba City, and had a job on the railroad for three years. Then he said he had a letter for me, that had been sent care of the wholesaler in Gallup. He grinned and said, "How's Callie? She old friend of mine."

My heart began to hammer when I saw her name on the return address. "Callie Allison, Palace Bar, Prescott, Arizona Territory." I went around behind the warehouse and found a patch of sun, and sat on an old wagon seat there.

She wrote:

DEAR LINK,

I bet you're surprised to hear from little ole me!!! Link, I have to see you and I can't write it in a letter because Mr. Beasley is likely to get it when it gets there and believe me he will read it. I hope you did not pay him any money yet and if you did, why, get it back. So I am coming up there. It is my fault you are there and I would feel awful if you got cheated by that old Skin Flint. I got homesick for the old place after you left and thinking how nice it would be to see it again and you there, too. Maybe

I shouldn't say it, but maybe most of the reason is I miss you a lot. I mean outside of wanting to warn you before you let any money get out of your hands. I will get to Gallup on the train on the 16th. Can you meet me with a wagon? Go to McLean's grocery warehouse. I'll go there every morning if you aren't there to meet me.

Love and Kisses
XXXXX!
CALLIE ALLISON

I got so excited I ran into the store to tell Beasley I needed his wagon. But then I stopped and calmed down, because I couldn't start that day. I had to get together food and blankets, and grease the wagon and check over the harness.

Old Beasley looked up from the counter and said, "What the hell bit you?" He looked at the letter in my hand. "You just win a lottery or something?"

I said, "Can I use your wagon? I gotta go to Gallup tomorrow."

"You got a horse."

"I'm gonna pick up Callie. She's coming here."

"Comin' here? Well . . . I ain't just sure I want her here."

"Well, she comes or I go. And there goes your five thousand cash, and you can sit here and tend your rheumatism all winter. And next winter, and the one after."

He blinked and chewed his ragged old mustache. "What's she comin' here for?"

"She's homesick for you!" I said, and grinned at him. I was joshing, but he took me serious.

"Hohonya! Maybe she's homesick, but not for an old man like me."

I could see how flattered he was.

"Callie comin' back," he said to himself. "Well, it would be nice to see her again."

"So how about the team and wagon?"

"It'll cost you ten." Then he kind of snarled at me, "But you get this straight! I'm no Christer, but I got some morals. There ain't gonna be no runnin' back an' forth nights between your bedroom an' hers! You two ain't gonna make no hoorhouse outa the Ram House Tradin' Post!"

First, he'd been telling me how wild she used to be, then he'd made all sorts of excuses for her, and it was plain as the big nose on his face how pleased he was to have her coming back . . . then again, he couldn't trust her to behave. All of which sure had me puzzled. But then, he was an old man that had maybe been alone too much, maybe he had an old man's dirty mind, and maybe he was jealous of me. I was too excited to start worrying about his state of mind.

I greased the wagon and oiled the harness. Beasley's team was a lot better than the Navajo teams, and his heavy wagon had bows, a good canvas cover, and a spring seat. I grained the team good and took a sack of barley and a keg of water, and threw sheepskins and eight blankets into the wagon. Gallup was a hundred miles, three days each way at best, if I didn't hit bad weather or mud. I was in a sweat to get there. But I sure wasn't going to be in any hurry coming back, with just me, Callie, and that stack of sheepskins and blankets in the wagon box.

I bought a suit of wool long johns from Beasley because the ones I'd been living and sleeping in were taking a permanent set in the seat and the knees, and I guess they were a little high. I thought about taking the money, but then I thought it would be safer right where it was, and I only put thirty dollars in my wallet.

When I started next morning, the team was full to go, blowing their breath like steam jets. I had to hold back from pouring on the leather, I was so anxious to cover that hundred miles. They trotted a good deal without me whipping them. I pulled up and camped that night just off the road that went to Fort Defiance, where it turned off from the south rim of Canyon de Chelly. I'd passed half a dozen wagons that had climbed up out of the canyon, loaded with blankets, kids, cook pots, and sheepskin bedding, heading for their winter hogans because the winters were too tough down in the canyon, and there was too much danger of spring floods.

I made Fort Defiance the next night, but cooked out and slept in the wagon, and went on at daylight. I pulled into Gallup late the next afternoon, on the sixteenth, right on the dot, and found out where McLean's warehouse was. The train hadn't got in . . . a washout or something. It was an awful letdown. I pulled out of town and camped in the wagon again. I couldn't sleep much, though, and just before daylight, the train pulled in at the depot.

By the time I got harnessed up and drove to the depot, she wasn't there, but I found her waiting at McLean's. I grabbed her and kissed her, and she said, "You stop that! What will people think!" But she was laughing, and McLean and a couple of Indian swampers were grinning. She really didn't care. Her cheek was cold and soft, and when I hugged her I could feel her shape under her wolf skin coat. We had breakfast at some place I don't remember. I don't remember what I ate, either, because I couldn't keep my eyes off her.

We got her suitcase and carpetbag from the depot, and started out. I drove slow, because I didn't want to get as far as Fort Defiance, where some officer's wife would probably put her up in a room for the night.

While we drove, she hung onto my arm and pushed herself up against me, and the horses went along without any driving, because I sure wasn't paying them any mind.

After a while, she said, "Did Beasley sell you the post? I hope you haven't paid him anything."

"Why, no. We've been haggling, sort of, but he wants sixty-five hundred. Say, when I got there, he acted like he hadn't ever thought about selling out. Said he couldn't figure out why you said that."

"Why, the old liar! Everybody knows he's been wanting to sell. He's just trying to keep the price up, Link. He's awful sharp. I hope you've got the money with you."

"No. It's in a good safe place. I didn't want to have that much on me. Somebody tried to dry-gulch me before I even got to Jerome, after I left Prescott."

"Oh, Link! No!" She hugged me and said, "Are you all right? I couldn't stand it if anything happened to you!"

"He missed me. I think maybe I touched him up a little. You didn't see anybody in Prescott with a hole in him, did you?"

"No, I didn't. Did you see who it was?"

"No, I couldn't make him out. It could have been anybody. Maybe Harry Peters or Johnny Moore. The whole town knew I sold that section to Moyers. What was that in your letter about not paying Beasley anything?"

"Well, somebody said Beasley never did own the Ram House Trading Post. He's supposed to be just running it for somebody else, for board and room and a small salary. I think he's trying to cheat you. He could take the money and just disappear. And I'd feel just awful if I sent you up here and then you lost your stake. I had to come and find out, Link. And I couldn't write it to you for fear he'd get the letter."

"You went to all that trouble for me? Was that the only reason you came?"

She turned her head away and ducked down into her fur collar. "That was only part of it, Link. I missed you something awful. Kept thinking about you, and that time in your hotel, and . . ."

She was blushing, and I put my hand under

her chin and turned her face to me, and she let me kiss her.

"Callie, you are going to marry me, aren't you? And we'll run the post together, like we said? There's nothing else in the world I want, Callie."

She patted my cheek. "You're sweet, Link! But you mustn't rush me. I have to think it over. It's awful tempting and I, well, I'm awful fond of you, but ... well, let's get you settled first, if you really want to buy the post, and then we'll see. I used to help Beasley around the post, and I know where he keeps the books and the correspondence. I thought if I could maybe get a look at letters and books, I could find out for sure if he really owns the post, or if he's just out to cheat you."

When we camped a few miles south of Fort Defiance, I pulled off the road into a clump of juniper. I wouldn't let her cook or anything, but I got supper and served it to her like she was a queen. She was laughing, and saying how wonderful it was to be back on the reservation, and how she had always been homesick for it, and it was like coming home again.

But when I made up the bed in the wagon box, she made me pull it apart and make up two beds. In that narrow wagon box, they

105

were pushed right together side by side, but she made me fold the blankets lengthwise so the folds were between us, so I couldn't sort of slip into her bed. She let me kiss her goodnight before she got into the wagon and got her nightgown on and got wrapped in the blankets . . . and that's all she'd let me do except hold her hand.

It just about drove me frantic lying there so close I could feel her shape against my side. But she said she trusted me, and it wasn't like the night in the Brinkmeyer Hotel in Prescott, because she was thinking seriously about marrying me, and she wanted it to be right. I finally got to sleep, along toward morning.

Well, the next night was the same thing. We slept side by side, with about four layers of blankets between us. I got a little more sleep, but not much.

After we got started the next day, I thought of something, and pulled up. I said, "Hey, wouldn't they know at Fort Defiance whether Beasley really owns the post, or who he's working for – who has the license? We should've asked, back there."

"Oh, why didn't I think of that! Of course they would!"

"Well, I'll turn around. We'd ought to find out. Maybe we'll get snowed in if we go on to the Ram House, and not be able to get back to Fort Defiance." I grinned at her, and said, "It'll give me two or three more days out here with you, too."

"Oh, Link, let's keep going. I'm tired, and I need a bath and a change. I can still look at his books and letters and find out. Anyway, real winter doesn't start till January. We can go to Fort Defiance any time."

So I drove on, and we pulled into the Ram House Trading Post after dark. It was all lit up, and Old Beasley came out with a lantern, and fussed around while I helped Callie down. She patted his cheek and said, "Hello, Pops! Glad to see me?"

He hugged her shoulders. "Sure am!" he said. "C'mon in!"

We went in, and I built up the fire in the kitchen. Then went out and brought in the things, unhitched and put the team in the corral, and made sure they had hay and water.

When I came back in, she had opened a can of beef stew, stirred up a batch of biscuits, and made a pot of tea, and we sat there eating and thawing out. It made me think how wonderful it was going to be, after a day in the store, and the door locked, and just her and me sitting there by our fire, talking before we went in to bed. Beasley sat there grinning at her and asking questions that she answered

107

without telling him much.

He finally went out to the two-holer and came back and told Callie which room was hers – between his and mine – and went to bed.

I got up to get blankets for Callie, but she said she knew where things were, and got four of the Pendletons I'd brought back into the store, and made up her bed. Then she shut her door, and I sat by the stove, hoping she'd come out and kiss me goodnight.

Pretty soon, I heard her whispering in the hall, and I got up and went there. She was outside her open door, in her nightgown, with a big, soft robe around her, and fur slippers on. She put her fingers to her lips and whispered, "You better show me where you hid your money. You'll be helping out in the bull pen, or down at the corral part of the time, but I'll be around here and keep my eye on it. Beasley will sure find it, or his hired help will. You don't know them, him or those Navajos, either. You can't trust a one of them!"

"But, Callie! You sure don't think *he* would . . . !"

She put her arms around me and whispered, "Don't trust him, Link!" Then she kissed me, and I could feel her all soft and round when her robe fell apart in front and there was nothing between us but that thin nightgown.

And just then Old Man Beasley's door slammed back and he came limping out in his red long johns. He screeched at her, "You Goddamn' painted hoor! Not an hour in my house an' already you get down to work, huh? There ain't gonna be no fornicatin' nor carryin' on in my place. Don't you think for a minute I forgot anything about you! You behave like a Goddamn lady or I'll kick you the hell outa here . . . in the middle of the night, if I have to!"

I was about ready to slug him, and I thought she would start clawing his eyes out, but all she said was, "I didn't do anything, Mr. Beasley. You've got the wrong idea. Just because my father used to accuse me of all kinds of dirty things . . ." and she began to cry and went into her room and shut the door.

"I oughta knock your Goddamn china teeth down your throat! Don't you ever talk like that again!"

He glared at me for a minute, then mumbled something and went into his room and shut the door.

In bed, I laid there thinking of Callie all warm and sleepy, not twenty feet away, and I could hardly stand it not to get up and sneak into her room. And I thought: Why that dirty-minded old fart! At his age! Jealous

of a girl that could've been his granddaughter!
Well, I hope I never get that bad off!

CHAPTER 7

While the old man and I were having
breakfast, Callie came out. She had on a
long-sleeved dress, a skirt that came to the
floor, and no paint on her face. I thought
she looked prettier than ever. She acted
like nothing had been said last night, but
Beasley wouldn't talk to her. He got up
and left without his second cup of coffee.
But by afternoon, he seemed to have forgot
his blow-up last night, and was smiling and
talking with her. Callie wasn't one to hold
a grudge, and everything was all right again
between them. He grinned at me a couple
of times, but I was still sore and wouldn't
talk to him.

For the next few days, Callie helped us in
the bull pen, and when Beasley's rheumatism
flared up, he'd go in and lay down and let her
run the store. Some of the Navajos smiled at
her, but others, mostly the old ones, wouldn't
say anything to her, and waited till Old Man
Beasley would come out and wait on them.

She knew where everything was, and kept the accounts up to date on the paper sacks. She and Franklin Yazzie helped me a lot, showing me how to run things.

Then when Yazzie said he had to go to a Sing they were having for a sick friend of his up by Lukachukai, Beasley told him to go ahead, that Callie and I could handle things all right. Yazzie saddled up and rode off.

Beasley took to his bed again that afternoon, and when we heard him shut his door, Callie said, "I haven't had a chance to get a look at his books or letters, to find out if he really owns the place or not. And he's got all the correspondence and records under his bed, in a trunk."

"Look," I told her, "I don't know any reason why he'd lie to us. He's been here thirty years. What makes you think he'd just work for wages all that time? Did you ever know anybody to come around and check up on him?"

"No, not while I was here. But I heard down in Prescott that he sold out a couple of years ago, and he's just holding on now till the new owner can settle his affairs and come and take over. Link, you don't know him. He's crooked as a dog's hind leg. Don't you trust him. Don't make a deal with him till I can find out."

"Well, all right. Whatever you say. But, Callie, we can't hang around here forever. We could get snowed in and be here all winter, and maybe not be able to buy the place after all. I want to get started on something else, if I can't buy the post."

"You just trust little ole Callie. I'll find out," and we left it at that.

The Navajos were getting friendlier with me, and I was learning a few Navajo words. They'd laugh like hell when I tried to say them, and I'd laugh, too, and it seemed to sort of break the ice.

Callie did a lot of joking with the young bucks, and there were more of them coming to trade since she came. Some of the girls and young women were real pretty, but they were all bashful, and not one of them would talk to me at all, even when they'd been to school at Tuba City and could talk English.

I used to think Indians never smiled or cracked jokes, but after they got used to me a little, they were always laughing and playing jokes on one another. I really began to like those people, and I was surer than ever that I'd have the best life here a man could want, specially if Callie said the word. I was sure, now, she was going to, if I could just buy the place.

One night at supper I was asking questions

and they were both telling me about the Navajos, and I said, "They're sure dirty, though! All those sateens and velveteen and jewelry; you'd think they'd wash once in a while ... their faces and hands, if not those fancy clothes."

Beasley got mad. "You think you'd look like you just stepped out of a turkish bath if you had to drive a wagon maybe twenty miles to the nearest water, and the water muddy at that? And if you had to build you a house out of logs or rocks with your own hands, and a dirt floor, and the hogan full of smoke all the time? And nothin' but an open fire to cook on? And no soap, bath tub, or towels? Listen, they take a sweat bath all the time, even in winter, in a little hogan they built. Put hot rocks in, and pour water on 'em and sweat the dirt off. And the men and boys take a roll in the snow, naked, every morning in the winter."

I said, "Don't get sore! I guess I'd be dirtier than them if ...."

But he was still fired up. "You take a good look at their hair? You seen how clean it is, every one of 'em? They pound up yucca root an' make suds an' wash their hair, an' wash each other's hair with it. You'd ought to keep your eyes open!" He was still sore at me when he went to bed.

The next day, Mary Wilson came with her team and wagon. When she came inside, Callie ran up to her, held out her hand, and said, "Why, Mary! I didn't know you were back!"

Mary said, "Hello, Callie," like she wasn't much interested, and she didn't shake hands. She didn't pay any attention to me at all, but I didn't mind. I didn't want Callie to get the idea that I was interested in any Indian girl.

Mary had a long list of things to buy – flour, salt, sugar, baking powder, canned goods, bacon, and the like. I knew the stock pretty good by then, and I got the stuff off the shelves when she read the list, and piled it by the door. Callie started to write it on a paper sack, but Mary paid cash.

Old Man Beasley came out and said, "Hello, Adezhbah! How you been?" and began to rattle off the Navajo.

She smiled at him, shook hands, and talked Navajo to him. Then I helped her carry the stuff out to her wagon, and watched her drive off. When I went in, Callie acted like she was mad at me. I guess she didn't like having me help Mary.

"Mary Wilson!" she said. "She's not even Navajo, she's a half-breed! Putting on airs just because she went to college. Believe me, she's no better than she ought to be! We grew up together, and where does she think she gets off making herself out better than anyone else!"

Beasley said, "Because she damn well is!"

Callie said something under her breath so he didn't hear her . . . but I did . . . "You Goddamn old fart!"

I was shocked. But I guess you can't be a singer in a saloon and not learn some bad words, and if somebody makes you mad enough, why then . . .

By the time we locked up, she had cooled down. Old Man Beasley stayed in his room. His rheumatism was acting up, and I took him a bowl of mutton soup Callie had made up, and some soda crackers, and helped Callie get our dinner. Before we got through, we could hear the old man snoring, and I tiptoed down the hall, and closed his door.

Something had been bothering me, and I was scared to bring it up, but finally, I said, "Callie, Beasley said when you ran away from your father down in Phoenix, you went with some man. I kind of wondered . . ."

She looked at me sideways and her face got red. She said, "He's got a nasty mind, Link, and he doesn't like me. I was going to tell you, if I decide to marry you. It wasn't like he said. I didn't have any place to go, and nobody to turn to, and I couldn't stand it with my father any more. You wouldn't believe what he was like, and how mean he treated me. Never believed anything I said, and kept accusing me of, well, of sleeping with the Navvie boys. And I didn't, Link. You know I wouldn't. And down in Phoenix, this man was awful good to me. I married him, Link. I wouldn't go with him any other way. And it didn't last, not six months, and I divorced him. And by then I began to get jobs singing in the saloons – he got the first one for me – and I managed to make my own living. And now I don't ever want to talk about it again. I don't want to remember it. And if this makes any difference, why I just can't help it, Link. It happened, and I can't change it."

"Listen," I said. "I'm not so lily-white myself. And I can sure see how it was. It doesn't change a thing. Callie, I love you, and I want to marry you. I think Beasley's coming around. And if I can buy the place, why . . . you like it up here, don't you? And we can run it together, make a good thing out of it, and have us a real good life."

She reached across the table and took my hands. She was crying, but not making any noise about it. She said, "Link, I never knew a man as wonderful as you. That thinking about my being married once was the only thing stopping me. I thought you'd . . . well,

I was afraid to tell you, but I knew you'd find out sometime. I think I will, Link."

I started to get up and go around the table, but she said, "No, Link. Hold off a little while. We've got to be sensible. If you can buy the place, all right. But, look ... I wish it was different, but if he won't sell, you'll run through that money. And I already told you I can't marry any forty-a-month cowboy. I just can't do it, Link!"

"That's all right, Callie. I'll buy the place if it takes every cent. And I can wait, now I know."

"We'll know pretty soon."

"Know what, Callie?"

"Know whether he owns the license. Before I left Prescott, I wrote to a man I know in the Bureau, and he'll look it up." She got up then and kissed me, and went to bed.

Two men from the Bureau of Indian Affairs came in a wagon the next day, and spent a while with Beasley in his room. He was feeling better that day, and we all had dinner together. They stayed overnight in the spare bedroom, and left in the morning. I didn't get a chance to ask them if Beasley owned the post. A missionary came in that day, a sour, pinched-looking man that was working on the Hopis in Old Oraibi. Beasley wasn't very friendly, but polite enough. And the next day a packer came in with two tourists, and a couple of pack mules. They'd been up to Ram House Ruin for a week or so, but it got too cold for them. They had a few old pots, and a piece of woven cloth they'd dug up. After having lunch with us, they left for Chinle, and then on to Gallup to catch the train. I was glad about all the visitors. I thought if they came in like this it would keep Callie from being lonesome after we were married, and would sort of break up the monotony for both of us. When they left, Beasley told me a Navajo had told him there was somebody camping in Sheepdip Wash. Maybe a prospector, Beasley thought, but he said whisky runners came sometimes, and made a hell of a lot of trouble. Or maybe somebody hiding from the law. I could see it worried him, so I said if he wanted, I'd ride over tomorrow and see if I could find the man. Callie told me not to go, that I might run into trouble. But old Sox needed exercise, and I hadn't had a chance yet to look the country over.

So I saddled up in the morning and cut across country toward Sheepdip Wash, thinking I'd keep out of sight. Maybe I'd get a look at the camper, and if he looked all right, go in and talk to him.

Sox wanted to run, and I let him. Then we just wandered around and I never did get to

Sheepdip Wash, at least I didn't recognize it if we did, and I didn't see anybody or any camp. I visited a hogan for a while. Beasley had told me never to ride right in, but to stop a good ways off and let them see you. He said not to go in unless they came out and invited you. It turned out to be old Many Horses. I knew him from the store. His wife fed me stew, fried bread, and coffee, and he kept saying "Howdy do" and grinning whenever I said anything. I guess it's the only English he knew.

I had a good day, and then I got in a sweat to get back to Callie, and old Sox went into that single-foot of his and we got back before dark. Callie looked kind of tired and worried, and said Old Man Beasley had been in bed all day with his rheumatism, and the store had been busier than usual, and she hadn't even had time to eat. I pitched in and helped her with the last few customers, and we locked up.

She sat on a stack of rugs, slumped down, and said, "Link, could you get supper? I'm beat down."

I kissed her. "You bet! You go in and wash up and lay down till I call you."

She went to her room, and when I went down the hall, Old Man Beasley called to me from his room, and I went in.

"You find him?" he asked.

"No, I don't think I even found Sheepdip Wash."

"Well, never mind. If he's still around, the Navvies will see him. I'll hear about it."

I built up the kitchen fire, and went into my room. It didn't look quite right, somehow. My roll, tarp, and saddlebags had been moved around. I could tell by the dust under the bed that somebody had pulled them out. When I opened them up, I could see things had just been crammed back into the saddlebags. The roll was tied with a granny knot, and I always tied it with a running bowline on the lash rope, and a couple of half hitches. I moved the bed, but the brick hadn't been pulled out, and my money was still there.

I got supper and called Callie, and helped the old man to come to the table. When I asked Callie if anybody had gone back to the living quarters during the day, she said, "Why, not that I saw. But they might have. I couldn't watch everybody. Why?"

"Somebody went through my saddlebags and my bed roll."

"Why, how could you tell?" she asked. I told her about the messed up saddlebag and the granny knot.

"Did they get anything? Was anything gone?" I told her no.

120

She stared at Beasley, and said, "There wasn't anybody back in this part of the house but you! All day long, there wasn't!"

He didn't get mad, like I thought he would. He grinned at her kind of crooked. "If it had been me, Link would never see I was there. I'd've put everything back the way it was, and I know a granny knot when I see one. How about you, Callie?"

Callie argued, "You'd do that just to prove it was me! You'd tie a granny knot! You're just mean enough!"

"Quit talking foolish! It wasn't you and it wasn't him. With the bull pen full of Navajos all day, it could've been anybody."

"If Franklin Yazzie was here, I'd sure know who it was!" Callie said. "Maybe he came back and sneaked in through a window or something."

Beasley snorted and started to say something, and I said, "Let's drop it. They didn't get anything, and I'll find a new hiding place. That is unless you want the money right now, before somebody does steal it, and you never get a chance to sell out to me or anybody else."

"Well, I been thinkin' it over," he said. "I've about made up my mind. You gimme fifty-five hundred, and she's yours, the whole shebang. And I'll pull out tomorrow, and

121

then you can sleep double or do any damn thing you're a mind to, for all of me."

"Not quite so fast," Callie said. "What about the license? If you've even got one."

"What kind of foolishness is that? I've had one every year for thirty years. I'll show you." He started to get up.

"Well, even if you have, what about a license for Link? He sure isn't going to pay you something till he knows he can get one."

"That ain't hard. I got plenty of friends in the Bureau of the U.S.D.I. There won't be no trouble there."

"Well, you get at it, then. Go with him to Fort Defiance and get it fixed up. But you don't get paid till he has his license."

"You know I ain't in no shape to travel. I'll write him a letter, an' he can go."

"That won't do. Letters back and forth, forty miles to Fort Defiance, and maybe no wagon going or coming for weeks at a time, if we get a snow storm. No, we'll wait till you can go together. I'll mind the store."

Beasley looked at me. "Link, you gone deef an' dumb? Whose money is it, yours or hers?"

I didn't answer, and he said something in Navajo and went crippling out of the room.

Callie waited a while, listening, and pretty soon she said, "You better let me take care of the money, Link. He won't be up to traveling for a while . . . and after what happened this afternoon, it isn't safe."

A sudden thought popped into my mind, just out of nowhere, that I tried to push aside and not think about.

I said, "Whoever tried to find it knows it's not in my room, now. I think I'll leave it right there."

"You mean it is there somewhere, and they missed it? So they wouldn't search your room again. Is that it? Well, I can keep an eye on your room then. And I'll keep the door to the hall locked when I'm in the bull pen. And Beasley doesn't know where it is, either."

And for some reason I didn't stop to figure out right then, I said, "I didn't say it's in my room. I just said nobody will search there again." I could see that sounded pretty lame, so I said, "I'll put it somewhere else."

She gave me an odd looking smile. "Well, Linkie, you'll have to learn to trust me if you're going to marry me."

She came and sat on my lap. She put her arms around my neck, and kissed me good. "Mrs. Lincoln Conway! Sounds nice, doesn't it!"

My heart gave a big jump in my chest. "You mean you will? You're gonna marry me?"

"Yes, Linkie, I am."

123

Well, I hugged her hard, and started kissing her, and we both got pretty excited. When I got my hand inside her blouse, she didn't stop me, but that corset and all those underclothes sure got in my way.

But somehow, hot and randy as I was, that's all it was. And I seemed to be sort of standing aside watching us, like a third party. There wasn't any big thrill, no real joy – only the excitement of having my hand on the breast of a woman, and knowing she was getting excited. My mind kept shying away from admitting what was bothering me, but I knew what it was. I didn't trust her any more ... because she didn't love me. She loved my six thousand dollars, and she'd do anything to get it.

A little common sense began to take over, instead of just lust for her. I could see, now, she never showed any interest in me till I got the money.

Old Man Beasley really knew her, and he was pulled two ways. He remembered what a sweet little girl she'd been, way back, and he knew what had turned her bad. He knew what a rough time she'd had, and why, and that it really wasn't her fault. He was sorry for her, and didn't want to believe it any more than I did ... but he knew she was bad.

All the time this was running through my

mind and beginning to make me a little sick to my stomach, she was nuzzling my neck and pressing my hand against her breast. She kissed me on the ear and whispered, "The old bastard's asleep, Linkie. Come on! My bed's been awful cold and empty!"

I wasn't ready to throw any accusations at her, or even hurt her feelings, for that matter. I kissed her – and that almost gagged me – and I said, "He's got ears like a rabbit. He'd hear us for sure and come charging in like the Lord's avenging angel. We better not, Callie."

And I pushed her off my lap, and we stood up. I whispered, "Good night," and started to kiss her again, but she didn't put her arms up or lean toward me or anything. Just stood there with a funny little smile on her face and watched me walk to my room. I turned and looked back, and she was still watching me, with her hands on her hips and that crooked smile on her face.

I laid awake a long time, telling myself I was wrong, that I was worse than unfair to her, that I didn't have any proof, and that she had come all the way from Prescott to warn me about Old Man Beasley . . . but I wasn't wrong! And deep inside I knew it.

What I didn't know was just what I was going to do about it. She was shrewd, and the way she'd looked at me when I left her, she probably knew already what was bothering me. Maybe we could just let the whole thing drop without any fuss or name calling.

I finally got to sleep. When I woke up and smelled coffee and heard her rattling around in the kitchen getting breakfast, well, for a minute there I felt like jumping up, clicking my heels together, and hollering for pure joy. Then it came back to me, my thoughts last night, and my high spirits took a deep dive.

The arguments started up in my head again ... she hadn't ever really done anything to make me suspicious. She had only done nice things for me, coming with me to my hotel that night so I wouldn't get robbed, crawling into bed with me, there, giving me the whole idea about buying Ram House Post, then leaving a good job and coming all the way up here to watch out for me and keep me from getting cheated. I was an ungrateful, stupid fool!

Only I really didn't think I was a fool. Why should she fall in love with me all of a sudden? Why should she come all the way up here just to look out for my interests, and nothing in it for her? Why did she keep saying my money wasn't safe where I hid it, but I ought to let her keep it for me?

No! She was too pushy! Too itchy to find

126

out where I hid the money! Too anxious to get her hands on it!

The truth was, I didn't know what the hell to believe.

I got dressed and went out to the kitchen. She didn't smile, but just said, "Sit down and have your breakfast, Link."

I heard Beasley coughing. I went to his room, and he was bad off. He had some fever, his chest was sore, and his rheumatism was giving him hell. He grinned at me, though, and said he could see himself soaking up the sun in Santa Barbara, with flowers blooming and birds flapping around. I brought him the glass with his teeth, and he shoved them into place. For breakfast, he drank some coffee and ate a couple of pieces of bacon. Then he turned over and went to sleep.

After I ate, Callie said she'd watch out for him. I went down to the corral, forked hay out of the shed, and had to break the ice in the tank before I could haul water to the trough. Sox's fur was standing straight out, like the two team horses and a couple of Indian nags that belonged to Beasley. Sox was like a colt, pretending to kick at me and bucking around the corral. I was down there about an hour, and when I went back to the post, Callie had opened up. There were a couple of old long-hairs and a squaw drinking

127

pop and rolling cigarettes.

Callie looked worried and I said, "What's the matter?"

"The old Navvie there says Henry Roanhorse is real sick in his hogan. I don't know what to do. I can't leave, because you can't run the place alone. He ought to have help or we ought to bring him here until we can get word to Fort Defiance to send a doctor, or maybe take him there."

"What about them?" I asked, and nodded toward the two old bucks.

"They rode in. They didn't bring a wagon, so they couldn't bring him back here if he's bad off."

"I'd go if I thought I could find the place. Trouble is, I don't know my way around, yet."

"Oh, would you? Link, it would get you in real good with the Navvies if you'd help. I can tell you how to get there. It isn't hard, but it'll take you most all day. You better take food and blankets, and I'll send along some cough syrup and stomach pills. The main thing is to get him back here if he's real sick, where Beasley can help him. Beasley's done a lot of doctoring."

She got a pencil and paper, and began to draw a map. "You take the road toward Round Rock, and then take the right hand

128

fork. About ten miles farther, there's five or six hogans. That's Round Rock. You take the left fork there, and keep going. There's a deep wash running beside the road on your left, Lukachukai Wash, and right where it gets shallow and meets the road, you turn off and go straight east. You can't miss the turn, because there's an old dirt hogan there with a hole in the back wall, where somebody died. There's a wagon track to follow. Keep going to Hasbidito Creek, and there's two hogans there, one of the old dirt ones and a good log one. That's Roanhorse's."

It looked pretty complicated to me, but she said it was easy if I followed her map.

She put food, blankets, sheepskins, and medicine in the wagon while I harnessed the team. I got my carbine. When I climbed up, she said, "I've got to hurry back before those old men rob the place. Good luck, Link darling!" I started to ask her what she meant by that, but she went running back to the post.

I took the right fork to get to Round Rock, like her map said, and maybe an hour later I hadn't got to the next fork yet, and I saw a rider coming, A Navajo with a blanket wrapped around his legs and behind, and wearing one of those flat-brimmed, undented black hats and a greasy, old sheepskin coat.

I didn't recognize him till he pulled up and said, "Hey, Link, what the hell you doin' out here?"

It was Franklin Yazzie, coming back from the Sing. I said, "I'm glad you're going back. The old man's sick and Callie's running the store by herself."

"Oh, I ain't goin' back yet. There's a Squaw Dance clear over to Dennehotso. I'll be ridin' all night."

"How far is it to the turn-off for Hasbidito Creek?"

"Chris' sake! What you want up there?" and I told him Henry Roanhorse was sick and I was going to bring him back to the Ram House post.

"Well, he wasn't sick last night, nor for the last nine days. He was the Singer at the Nightway Chant for Bobby Begay, over at Lukachukai. Fixed Bobby up real good."

"Why, hell, that can't be right! They brought word to the post this morning!"

"Somebody havin' fun with you. Ol' man Roanhorse, he been at that Sing at Lukachukai nine days, him and his whole fam'ly. Well, so long, I gonna cut cross country here," and he whacked his spurs into the horse and cut away from the road.

I sat there wondering what to do. I couldn't think of a single reason why he'd lie to me.

We were pretty good friends. But I couldn't figure out why that old Navajo at the post would've lied to Callie, either, except just to stir up trouble. Then I thought rather than drive another ten, fifteen miles and find nothing, and drive all that way back, I'd better go back. I swung the team around and hit 'em a lick with the reins and they went into a trot.

We made it back in about two hours, about noon, and as we came over the rise that looked down on the post, three horses came galloping past, the two Indian ponies that were in the corral and – I could hardly believe my eyes – *my* horse, Sox! I yelled at him, and he shied and went off over the hill.

There was a man untying a saddled horse from the corral gate, and the gate was wide open. I stood up and yelled at him, and damn if he didn't pull a six-gun and take a shot at me! I let myself go and fell back over the seat into the wagon box and grabbed my carbine and jacked a shell into the breech. By the time I poked my head out from under the wagon cover, the team was acting up and getting tangled in the traces, jerking the wagon sideways, and the man was pouring in the steel, and goin' over the hill full gallop.

I tried to steady the carbine on the sideboard, but the team was still bucking and hauling sideways. I shot three times, but I didn't think I hit anything, and then he was gone out of sight.

The door of the post was wide open, and not a sound from there. I jumped down and jammed another cartridge into the breech and ran for it as hard as I could go.

CHAPTER 8

Old man Beasley was lying sprawled out in his nightshirt in front of the counter. His head was bloody. I heard him groan when I jumped over him and yelled, "Callie!" and ran through the kitchen and hall into Callie's room.

She wasn't there.

Then I heard her crying, in my room.

She was on the floor, all huddled up in a corner, with her shirtwaist half torn off her, and her hair all tangled, hanging down. She was kind of whimpering, and I kneeled down and got my arms around her. Her mouth and nose were bloody and swollen, and her left eye all red and swelled shut.

I hugged her tight and said, "Callie! My God, Callie!" and she tried to push me away,

132

and really howled, with tears rolling down her face and her nose running. I picked her up and laid her on the bed. There was blood on her shirtwaist . . . from her nose, or something worse.

"Are you hurt any place else?"

She kept on bawling and didn't answer, and rolled over so her back was to me.

I turned her back. "Are you all right?" and started to unbutton her shirtwaist to see if she was shot or had any broken ribs, but she kept pushing my hands away, and wouldn't look at me.

She mumbled, "Leave me alone!" and bawled louder than ever and rolled over and pushed her face into the pillow.

Then I heard Beasley swearing a blue streak, out in the bull pen. I didn't want to leave Callie, but she was still telling me to go away. I hurried out to the bull pen, and Beasley was up on one elbow.

I picked him up – he didn't weigh any more than her – and started to carry him to his bedroom, but he got to kicking and hollering at me to set him down, and I did. He was shaky on his feet, and his head was still bleeding, the hair all matted with blood over his left ear.

"Is he gone?" he said, and went into another string of swearing and saying, "That

133

bitch! That murdering hoor!"

Then Callie howled real loud, and he said, "Where's she at? and stumbled into the kitchen with me helping him, and we went to my room. I saw, then, that the bed was pulled away from the wall and the brick pulled out, and the hole was empty. My money-belt was gone.

He made a lunge for her with his hands hooked like claws, and I pulled him back and slammed him down into the chair.

He screeched, "She done it! She robbed you, an' near got me killed!"

I said, "You're crazy! You got a knock on the head! There was a man out there! Ran the horses off and rode out!"

"Yeah! They were in it together, only he left her holdin' the sack!"

I said, "Callie! For God sake!" and she blubbered and rolled over against the wall and wouldn't look at me.

Well, Beasley told me the whole thing. And at first I wouldn't believe him. But with what he said, and looking at her lying there sniffling and shaking, I knew it was true.

"He came a half hour after you left with the wagon. I was in bed, an' I heard it all. He told somebody to git the hell out – I guess there was some Navvies in the bull pen, an' he run 'em off. Then he say, 'What took you so God damn long gittin' rid of him! I been freezin' out there in the brush!' An' she says, 'I couldn't find out where he hid it till just yesterday. It's in his room.' An' they went to your room, an' I heard 'em pull the bed away from the wall. Then he says, 'Jesus! Pretty good! How much is it!' An' she says, 'He told me almost sixty-three hundred dollars.' "

Beasley had to stop, and lean back and close his eyes. I thought I ought to be fixing up his head, but I was so sick inside I wanted to puke. I was about to ask him who it was, even though I was pretty sure I knew, and he straightened up and went on. "Then the man says, real nasty, 'Well, kid, thanks for the help, an' all that. It's been nice knowin' you, you Goddamn hoor!' An' she began to screech, an' hollered, 'Ruby! What you mean? Ruby! You can't do this to me!' "

Beasley tried to spit at her, but it just dribbled down into his whiskers. And I could see the whole thing then, right from the start.

The old man said, "Then I could hear 'em strugglin' an' wallerin' around in there, an' her squallin' like a catamount, an' I got out of bed an' come into the kitchen. I never had no sense, I guess . . . keep my .45 out in the bull pen, hid in a paper sack under the counter. Oughta take it to bed, at night. I could hear him hittin' her, then. I guess he knocked her out, 'cause she shut up, an' he come out with your money belt. An' when he saw me, he pulled his gun. He says, 'I don't wanta hurt you, ol' man. Just keep the hell outa my way!' An' he shoved past me an' went into the bull pen. I grabbed the back of his shirt, an' he was swearin' an' cursin, an' hit me with the gun."

I took him into the kitchen, got a rag and hot water, and cleaned him up. There was a big lump over his ear, and I put some salve on it and bandaged his head. Then I went in and grabbed Callie by the arm. I hauled her off the bed, marched her into the kitchen, and shoved her into a chair. "All right! Let's hear the whole thing."

Well, she didn't have any spirit left at all. I guess Ruby beating her up like that, after she expected they'd go away together with a good stake, had really broke her up. She sat there like a lump, and told us.

I knew I ought to be getting after Ruby and not lose any time, but I was sick inside and still could hardly believe it. She kind of fascinated me, like a snake after a bird.

Between blubbering and blowing her nose, she said, "Ruby's the one I ran off with seven years ago down in Phoenix, like I told you. He was good to me, and I . . ."

I broke in and told her, "Get on with it!
136

Just tell me! Don't waste time!"

"We got married, and moved around a lot, Arizona and New Mexico and California, and he made me do a lot of bad things – getting men to come to my room and then he'd break in and find us and they'd pay him to keep quiet. And then when we came to Prescott, he said not to tell anyone we were married, and he got me the job in the Palace Bar."

"God damn you!" I yelled at her. "Get on with it! About me! About my money!"

She flinched back like I'd hit her, and I almost did.

"It was all his idea. I didn't want to do it, but he made me. I liked you, Link! But he was after your money from the start, and it was him that made me go to bed with you that night and tell you this place was for sale, so you'd take your money out of the bank."

"Then it was him that shot at me the day I left? Not Harry Peters or Johnny Moore?"

"I don't know anything about that," she blubbered. "He didn't tell me anything about trying to shoot you."

"Well, I believe that much, anyhow. If he'd've shot me and got the money, you'd never have seen him again."

"But it was Ruby that had me write you the letter, and come here and find out where you hid the money, and keep you from giving it to him." She nodded her head toward Beasley.

She had to stop and blow her nose again. "He was afraid Beasley would get it and leave, and we wouldn't be able to find him."

"Then he came up here, because you hadn't sent word that you found my money." And she said yes, and he camped in Sheepdip Wash and every day he'd sneak over to watch the place, hid out in the brush.

"And you had some kind of signal, after you found out where the money was?"

She nodded. "I hung some washing out on the clothes line where he could see it this morning. And he saw you take the wagon and go." She looked up at me with one eye purple and swelled shut, and the other one leaking tears. "But I was so glad to get away from him, after I got here . . . and Link, it got so I wasn't pretending. I fell in love with you. I really did, Link!"

Old Man Beasley said, "Jee-sus Christ!" and spit on the floor.

I started out through the bull pen, and she came scrambling after me, if you'll believe it, and got her arms around me. "Link! Oh, Link! I didn't mean to . . . You hate me, don't you! Where you going, Link?"

I turned around and put my hand in her face and shoved. She stumbled backwards and fell into the chair and put her face down in her hands and bawled.

In my bedroom, I got the spare box of shells for my carbine. I picked up my saddle, bridle, and saddle blanket, and went out.

I'd have still be on that wild goose chase Callie sent me on, trying to find Henry Roanhorse's hogan, if I hadn't run into Franklin Yazzie up by Round Rock. Ruby Blair would have had a ten-hour start. But as it was, he was only a few minutes ahead of me. He had a damn good horse, though, and the only thing left for me was Beasley's wagon team.

I looked around, but Sox wasn't in sight, and I didn't waste any time trying to find him. I unhitched the team, putting one of them in the corral, and saddling the other. He was sure no saddle mount – about fourteen hundred pounds, I guess. I had to let out the cheek straps of Sox's bridle for him. I put my carbine in the boot, got on and started down the road. I got the big plug into a trot by kicking him in the ribs. That was all I could do, because I forgot my spurs and my gloves, too, when I ran out of the post. I'd never catch up to Ruby, but I had to try.

There was no trouble following him. Outside of Sox and Beasley's team, his was the only shod horse for miles

139

around. He could hit for Ganado and from there go east to Gallup or west to Winslow, and catch the train. Or maybe he'd leave the road and go cross country to Flagstaff, or even make a switch and cross the Colorado at Lee's Ferry. I didn't think he'd do that, though. I figured he'd catch the train at Gallup, and I could follow and do the same thing.

I tried to keep my mind on Ruby and what I'd do if I caught up with him somewhere, it didn't matter when or where. If I had to shoot him to get my money back, I'd do it. But I was sure torn up inside about Callie. I could hardly believe she had turned out even worse than I'd suspected last night ... cheat, liar, thief, and still married to that son of a bitch gambler. And worse yet, what she'd done to me. All the sweet talk, even going to bed with me, and all the time just scheming to get her hands on my money and give it to that bastard.

Well, he stuck to the road for Ganado, not trying any tricky stuff like hiding his trail, just going at a steady lope, knowing he could outrun me, I guess.

What messed him up was that I'd got lucky. One of my shots had hit his horse – a lung shot – and I found it lying in the road, bleeding at the mouth. He'd stripped off the saddle and bridle and cut off through the brush on foot. I shot the horse.

There was a thin column of smoke way over past some juniper covered hills, in the direction he'd gone, and I rode along his tracks. They were deep in the sand, from the weight of his saddle.

In less than a mile, I came onto a hogan and a corral. When I rode up, a woman ran into the brush. The hogan door was closed. I yelled, "Ruby, come out of there!" but there wasn't any answer. I had my six-gun in my hand, and I got down, swung the door back, and charged in like a damn fool.

I tripped over something, and went flat on my face, almost into the hot coals in the fire pit. I'd stumbled over an old Navajo lying just inside the door – shot in the stomach. He was blood all over, and dead.

I went out and found Ruby's tracks at the gate of the corral, where there were two shaggy Indian ponies. I hollered for the woman, but she didn't answer and I led Beasley's horse into the corral and stripped off my saddle and bridle. Those ponies sure didn't want anything to do with me, but they were rope broke, and when I got one of them cornered and flipped the end of my reins over his neck, he stood still.

He was only about half the size of Beasley's horse, and I had to shorten the cheek straps of the bridle again. When I led him out and closed the corral gate, I heard a horse coming through the brush. I looped the reins around a gate pole and laid down.

An Indian kid about twelve years old rode up bareback. I jumped up, and he jerked his horse around and kicked it in the ribs, but he stopped when I yelled at him and waved my gun.

I said, "What happened here? How long ago was it?"

"Man come, he got saddle," he said. "He take horse."

"How long ago? Which way'd he go?" but he didn't understand. I guess I talked too fast.

"I went to my uncle's hogan." He pointed over west by sticking out his lower lip. "My t'ree uncle an' two Dineh frien' go an' tryin' to catch that man. I come back. Where my mama?"

"Where'd they go? They didn't come here."

"They say he gonna go back to road. My uncle they go for Chinle. Maybe they get there before him. Where my mama?"

"She ran off into the brush. Listen, I'm

taking this horse. I've gotta have him. I'll bring him back."

He didn't say anything, and I cut a big circle and picked up what had to be Ruby's tracks, and put my pony into a run. The kid was right, or his uncles were – Ruby had angled back to the road and turned onto it. I hit into a gallop, not trying to save my horse for a long chase, because it had started to snow and I might lose his tracks if he left the road.

My new horse was small, but he was tough, and he settled into a steady lope. I walked him some, after while, to let him blow, then kicked him into a run again. About ten miles farther on, we passed the branch road that went a couple of miles to Chinle. A little past that, the tracks of five running horses cut in from the west to head him off. I saw where Ruby had hauled his horse up short and turned back and run off the road, going flat out. It was plain, then, those Navajos had cut him off. I followed the churned-up tracks and saw where two of the Navajos had split off and swung a little to the left of Ruby's tracks, and two others had cut to the right a little, and the other one kept right on his heels. Looked like they were hazing him straight through the brush for Chinle. Probably figured he'd run into more Navajos there, and they'd have him.

Well, that's what they did. Only he got there first, and went on straight through the scatter of hogans and out the other side before they could get ahead of him and get more help.

I stopped at Sam Day's trading post to ask where they might have gone. Day wasn't there. Bi-zah-dee, the Navajo helper, said the whole village saw this white man spurring like hell, and the five Navajos pounding along behind him. Two or three others got their horses and followed. He said they had him trapped if they could force him to go down into Canyon de Chelly, because there was only one rough foot-trail out, except the wagon road that went down into the canyon from right here, and only the Navajos knew where the trail was.

I rode on at a trot, and there was a wide trail with a lot of wheel tracks, going down into the canyon, and that's where they had chased Ruby.

It started gradually, an easy grade, and just kept going down and down, with the canyon walls rising higher and higher on each side. There was a half inch of snow by now. The canyon floor was white, and I felt like a little bedbug crawling on a sheet. Those cliffs were about a quarter of a mile apart, with some straight stretches and then long bends, with that flat, sand floor between. A stretch of cottonwoods with a few yellow leaves still on them ran along the bottom on both sides, and along the washes and arroyos that broke into the cliff face here and there. I began to see old ruins in caves and on ledges way up above, and one down almost on floor level. The sun was down below the south rim, now, and the shadow crawling up the north cliff. It was slow going, because the sand was loose and deep except along the shallow, frozen stream that twisted and branched and came together again. I passed a couple of hogans, but there wasn't anybody in them, no wagons, nor sheep in the pens. The cornfields and squash fields were stripped. Five horses came trotting around a wide bend, coming toward me, and shied when they saw me and cut across the canyon. They didn't make a sound in the sand, and all I could hear was the wind. Nothing else, till I heard the shots, way ahead down the canyon.

I kicked the horse then, and he ran . . . because I thought, if they've shot the son of a bitch they'll sure search him, and there goes my money!

The horse went buck-jumping along

making hard going of it in the sand, and we rounded a big bulge where a shoulder of the wall stuck out into the canyon, and ran right into the middle of seven Navajo riders. That is, it looked like seven at first, but there were two on one horse, eight altogether. They were all around me in a second, and every one of them had a gun pointed at me.

One of them was a kid not much older than the one at the hogan where Ruby Blair killed his father. He said, "Where you got my brother' horse?"

I put my hands up and said, "Hold on, now! I didn't steal the horse. I traded him. I'm after that man you were chasing."

He kicked his pony up beside me and shoved the carbine into my ribs. "That Hosteen Lichee horse! Maybe you friend that fellah we go after, huh?"

Then he recognized me, and let up a little. "You Link, from Ram House, huh? What you do here?"

"That man nearly killed Old Man Beasley and Callie. He shot your brother, too. You see him on past here? Who did the shooting?"

The others crowded in close, talking. I guess they were asking the kid what I said. One of them had a piece of his ear gone, and blood was running down his neck. The kid talked to them, then asked me, "You seen my brother Hosteen Lichee?"

I didn't want to tell him, but I guess he knew. "He's dead." His face didn't show what he thought. He told the rest of them, and they growled and stirred around.

The kid told me, "We almos' catchin' him, but he get behind big rock. That where Canyon del Muerto come into Canyon de Chelly. He shoot at us. He kill one horse. We comin' back, then."

I couldn't blame them much. A man with a fast-shooting Winchester forted up behind a rock, and maybe no cover for them, and night coming on.

"He gotta stay in canyon," the boy said. "Can't get out. Some time he gotta come out where he come in. We gonna get him when he do that."

"You mean a man can't climb out anywhere?" I asked.

"Oh, one trail, but he don't know that one. An' we gonna have one man watch that place, where it come out on top."

"Maybe the Navajos living down here will get him, or at least find out where he is."

"Everybody gone," the kid said. "All Dineh take sheeps and horse and wagon and

147

go out before snow. Go to other hogan. Nobody here no more."

"Well, hell, he can live all winter down here. Just use somebody's hogan. Plenty of firewood, maybe corn stored up, rabbits and deer and such."

"No, he don't," the kid said. "He gotta have fire, and we see smoke where he is at."

"Don't Canyon del Muerto join up with Canyon de Chelly down there someplace? You know which one he took?"

"That big rock, they say Junction Rock, that where he shoot at us," he said. "Right there, that where Canyon del Muerto come in. If he not crazy, he not goin' up Canyon del Muerto. That one very bad." He made motions with his hand, showing how rough the canyon was. "Few miles up there, horse not go no more."

"How far is this Junction Rock?"

He didn't know how to say it in yards or miles. He said, "Half hour on horse," but I didn't know whether he meant walking or running. "You go there? You don't got no blanket. Plenty cold tonight. Maybe snow."

I said, "He's gotta hole up somewhere, and he's gotta have a fire. Maybe I'll smell smoke. I'm not as sure as you that he couldn't

148

find his way out tomorrow. I never saw a canyon yet a man couldn't climb out of on foot."

"You been down here before?"

"Not here," I said, "but I been in a lot of canyons."

The others were asking him questions, and I guess he was telling them that I was going after Ruby, even if it was freezing and I had to stay all night in the canyon.

One old buck said, *"Doh-haly-ahn! Doh-haly-ahn!"*

The kid said, "He say you crazy."

Then without any signal or anything, they all kicked their ponies and moved off at a trot, heading back out of the canyon.

Sitting there that few minutes, I got chilled through. My blanket-lined coat didn't come much below my waist, and I'd run off without my gloves. My fingers were so stiff I could hardly tie my bandanna around my ears.

The sun was gone from the canyon, now, and there were clouds driving past. I put my hands under my arms and kicked the pony, and he trotted ahead. After while a great big rock loomed up through the snow. It must have been five hundred feet high, like a big square building. Behind it I could make out the shape of the cliffs against the sky – the sloping, broken walls of Canyon del Muerto

149

bearing left and the straight-sided, sheer walls of Canyon de Chelly going to the right. It had stopped snowing, but it was getting dark, and I couldn't see much else except the flat floor of Canyon de Chelly, bright with the white sand and powdering of snow. The wind was like ice. I knew I'd been a damn fool not to go back to Chinle with the Navajos, and come back down in the morning. There was no way to tell whether Ruby had gone up Canyon del Muerto or Canyon de Chelly . . . or maybe whether he'd just stayed behind Junction Rock and let me go past. But I had something else to think about now.

I kept on up Canyon de Chelly because I figured the going was easier than Canyon del Muerto, and I was afraid to try to go all that way back to Chinle in the dark. It was almost pitch dark now and I had to find a hogan or a cave where I could get out of the wind and build a fire.

The moon came out again and lit things up, but a cloud would sail past it and I couldn't see a thing till the moon came clear again. I rode on for a long time, and then got down and walked along under the north wall as close as I could get to the thickets of cottonwoods that grew along the bottom. I was warmer walking. There was less wind close to the trees and the wall. If I found a hogan, it would be in the cottonwoods, I thought. The horse kept stumbling into shallow washes when the moon was dark, and I was really worried now. I didn't even have an ax so I could cut some wood or build a branch shelter from the wind.

The moon came out again and lit up the cliff – a thousand feet straight up. There was a big white patch on the wall, maybe a hundred feet above the canyon floor. It looked like somebody had gouged a little piece out of the flat wall . . . but it only looked little, because that cliff was so big. The gouge would have had to be three hundred feet long and a hundred feet high. And in the middle of it was a big building. It looked like it might have been built last week, it was so perfect . . . at least as far as I could make out in the moonlight. It had a second story that was white, and in front of the gouge were some broken-down walls. I knew where I was, at least, not that it would do me any good. I was looking up at the White House Ruin.

I led the horse into the cottonwoods at the bottom of the cliff and started feeling around for cottonwood limbs or any kind of firewood. I could leave the horse down here behind those old walls for shelter, and if I got up into that ruin I could start a fire.

Then I heard a dog bark, over across the canyon, maybe five hundred yards. I looked over there and saw sparks rising, and I could smell smoke. So Ruby already had his fire! And maybe he'd be hugging that fire, half asleep as the heat got to him, half blind from the firelight, and I'd come out of the dark.

I tied the horse and beat my hands together to try to warm them up. I waited till a cloud went over the moon. Then, I started to angle across the sand to get under the cliff on that side, a hundred yards or so from where I'd seen the sparks. I figured I could sneak down to him in the shadow of the trees.

When I was halfway across, with my cold gun cocked and freezing my hand, two dogs came running at me, just raising hell. I thought, what the hell is he doing with dogs? I ran, then, with the dogs snapping at my heels but not brave enough to really jump me.

I got into the trees, and picked up a branch and shied it at one of the dogs. It yelped like I'd killed it and ran back, and barked at me from a distance. The other one kept circling around, just out of reach.

152

So Ruby was plenty warned. He'd be laying for me, and we'd play a little game of tag in the dark. I tried to get a bead on the dogs and stop their Goddamn yammering, and even things up a little between Ruby and me, but they didn't set still to be shot. All I could do was keep in the deep shadows and hope their barking would drown out any noise I'd make. I tried to wait till a cloud went across the moon before I moved, but the dogs kept bothering me and I damn near froze when I laid still. Then the moon came out, and I saw the hogan in a little clearing in the cottonwoods, maybe fifty yards out from the foot of the cliff. There was a corral and, I thought, two horses jumping around in it, boogered by all the racket. The other side of the hogan there was the frame of a summer shelter, crooked cottonwood poles with bare branches covering it. It wasn't going to be easy to get at Ruby, forted up in that log-walled hogan with a dirt roof a foot thick and just one little plank door about four feet high. But I sure couldn't stay out here and freeze.

I took a kick at one of the dogs, and he fell over backwards and barked like he was hysterical. I walked right up to the hogan and slid along it to the side of the door.

"Come on out with your hands up, Ruby. I got you cornered, and I'll just throw slugs through that door till I get you."

He didn't answer. I reached past the door frame and rapped on the door with the barrel of my six gun, and "Blam!" he shot through the door.

I tried to make myself move in front of that flimsy door and kick it down, but I could feel a lead slug ripping into my belly, and I couldn't make myself do it. We had a stand-off, all right, only he could wait it out and I couldn't.

"Ruby, you toss out my money belt and your gun, and I'll let you go. Because you're not coming out of there alive if you don't." My hand was getting so cold I wasn't sure I could pull the trigger.

Then somebody said something, inside the hogan. "What's that again?"

And somebody said, "What you want?" It was a woman's voice!

"Is Ruby holding you prisoner?"

And she said again, "What you want?"

Well, I knew if Ruby was there too, I'd never make it alive through that door, but I couldn't stay out here and freeze. I said, "Let me in. I'm not going to hurt you."

"Tell me who you are."

"I'm Link Conway. I been staying at the
154

Ram House Trading Post."

It was two or three minutes before the door swung open and I had a queazy feeling in my belly when I ducked down and went in with my gun in my fist. The fire had burned down to coals, but still there was so much light inside that I was kind of dazzled, so I didn't recognize her right away.

She was across the fire, backed up against the wall, holding an old Remington carbine pointed at my belly. It was Mary Wilson . . . Adezhbah.

CHAPTER 9

Her face didn't show a thing – only her eyes . . . scared and wide open. But she was shaking. She laid the Remington down and said, "You almost got shot."

"I'm sorry, I thought Ruby Blair had holed up in here."

"Who's Ruby Blair?" she asked.

I squatted down by the coals in the fire pit and warmed my hands. They were aching with the circulation coming back. I said. "It's Callie's husband. He robbed me, and beat her up and slugged Beasley with a gun."

She didn't say anything.

"That isn't all he did," I told her. "I shot his horse, and he took another one away from a Navajo . . . I think it's Hosteen Lichee. He killed Lichee to get the horse and Lichee's boy went and got some Navajos, his uncles and some others, and they took out after Ruby. They cut him off just past the Chinle road, and he made a run for it into the canyon here to lose them."

"But they didn't get him?"

"No. He's down here some place. I'm starved and half froze. You got anything to eat?"

"You got a horse? Put him in the corral. I'll fix you something."

That hogan was like the inside of an oven, and my cheeks and ears were tingling. I hated to go outside. The dogs raised hell again, but she yelled at them in Navajo and threw a chunk of firewood at them. They slunk off.

156

I walked across the canyon. The moon was covered by clouds, now, and it was black as pitch, not a light anywhere. I wouldn't have found the horse, only he snorted and lunged around when I blundered close to him. I untied him and led him across to Mary's corral, guided by the barking dogs and the sparks coming out of the smoke hole of the hogan. I put him in with her two horses.

When I went back into the hogan, it smelled like heaven. She had a big, black pot of mutton stew heating up, and was making fried bread. I put my saddle and saddlebags back against the rear wall.

I said, "I oughta feed and water the horse," and she dipped a bucket of water out of a barrel in the back, and said, "There's hay in the rack outside the corral."

When I came back in again and shucked off my coat, she served the stew and fried bread, and I stuffed myself. She sat there and didn't say anything, while I told her what Ruby Blair and Callie did, and why I had to get him.

Then she said, "Callie is no good. Not just because her father was mean to her, she's just made that way."

I wanted to ask her what she was doing down here when all the other Navajos had gone out for the winter, but the fire and the food was putting me to sleep. She told me when she heard the shooting down by Junction Rock, she'd been too scared to go out, and had stayed in the hogan with the door tied shut and her old Remington loaded. She said the dogs had been acting up, but it didn't necessarily mean Ruby had ridden on past up the canyon, because the dogs had been yapping ever since the shooting started, anyway.

I said I hoped he wouldn't freeze to death in a cave somewhere before I found him. I asked her, "You got any idea where he might hole in for the night?"

"I don't think we'll have a hard freeze, with the clouds blowing in, but we'll get some snow. There's a hundred places he could be ... ruins where he can build a fire, and empty hogans with plenty of corncobs to burn, and dried corn in storage bins to eat. Anyway, you don't know whether he went up Canyon del Muerto instead of here, or if he came this far."

"Well, he can't get out unless he goes back to Chinle. Those Navajos told me there's only one trail, and he doesn't know about it."

"It goes up the cliff about a hundred yards from right here," she said. "Just a trail the Navajos use sometimes, on foot. You'd never

158

get a horse up it."

"Well, they said they'd put a man to watch it, anyway," I told her. "And they'll be watching the head of the canyon, too."

"They won't do it. Too cold. And they'll never stay out after dark. They're scared of ghosts."

All this didn't make me feel very good about catching Ruby, but there wasn't anything I could do, now. I said, "I'm dead on my feet. Could you loan me a couple of blankets?"

"You mean in here?"

"Don't worry," I told her. "Even if I slept in here, I wouldn't bother you. But I'll wrap up outside somewhere out of the wind."

She gave me four big sheepskins that didn't stink, for a wonder, and two Pendleton blankets. She lit a coal oil lantern and helped me put some hay into her wagon – it still had the canvas cover on. She went back into the hogan without saying good night, and called her dogs in.

I made up my bed in the dark and pulled off my boots, gun belt, and hat, and pulled the blankets over my head. It seemed like it had got a little warmer, but maybe that was just because I'd thawed out. That bed was like a featherbed. I went to sleep right away.

When I woke up, there was an inch or more of wet snow. The sun was just hitting the top of the north rim, across the canyon, and there was no wind. It was a lot warmer than last night. The corral was muddy, and my pony and Mary's two horses looked miserable – soaking wet and steaming. Smoke was coming out of the hogan, stretching out in a flat layer.

When I pulled on my boots and got down from the wagon, the dogs growled at me. I stepped behind the wagon to do what I had to do, then carried the blankets and sheepskins to the hogan and knocked on the door.

Mary told me to come in, but she didn't look up when I opened the door. The coffee pot boiled over, and she took it off the fire and laid a round cake of dough in the frying pan. I ate two whole pieces the size of dinner plates, crisp, thick, and smoking with hot mutton fat, and had two cups of coffee loaded with sugar. I leaned back against the wall and rolled a smoke. "I sure do thank you for taking me in like this. Don't know what I'd've done."

She didn't say anything, and I watched her put her hair up in that big, long knot on the back of her head, and wrap it with about forty turns of white yarn. She was dressed the way I'd first seen her, and her skirts were wet around the bottom from going out into the snow.

"Can I pay you something?"

"No, that's all right. What are you going to do? Go back to the Ram House Trading Post?"

"I'm gonna look for Ruby. Ride down to Junction Rock and see if I can pick up any tracks."

"There's a lot of horses left down here for the winter. They've got no shoes, and his horse is the same. How'll you know his horse tracks?"

"Well, if I find tracks moving like they were going somewhere, I'll follow 'em. I don't think loose horses'll be stirring around in this weather, and the snow oughta help."

The inside of the hogan was clean as a whistle, in spite of the fire, ashes, and the dirt floor. There were two sacks of flour and a sack of sugar against the back, and some of her clothes hanging from the roof logs. There was a squaw saddle, a bridle with a lot of silver on it, canned goods, and coffee in Arbuckle's boxes stacked up to make shelves. The cooking pots were all black on the outside, but clean inside and stacked neatly. There were quite a few sheepskins, a stack of blankets, and two real good Navajo rugs. A lot more and better stuff than I'd seen in any other hogan, though I'd only been inside three or four.

I threw my smoke in the fire and got up. "Well, I'm going, Mary. Thanks a lot."

She didn't answer, and I picked up my gear, went out, and saddled the horse. I came back and got the water bucket. After watering him, and her two, I filled the magazines of the carbine and put it in the boot. When I rode off, she didn't come to the door. There was a sheep pen behind the hogan, with only four sheep in it, and a little dirt hogan out in back – the hogan for sweat baths, I guess. There wasn't any two-holer . . . but then, I never did see any hogan that had one.

I didn't have any idea at all where Ruby Blair might be, or if he was still in the canyon, or in Canyon del Muerto. I didn't try to hide or sneak through the cottonwood thickets, but rode across the canyon to see if I could cut any sign. I'd guessed wrong . . . four or five loose horses had been moving around, and their tracks criss-crossing, so horse tracks weren't going to tell me anything. I figured, too, that Ruby could have slipped past at daybreak, because I'd slept too long.

The snow was starting to melt even before the sun got down to it. I rode across to White House Ruin, and didn't see any tracks that weren't just wandering. I turned and rode back down Canyon de Chelly, thinking I'd see if there were any coming down Canyon del Muerto, or if he had gone up there last night, instead of up Canyon de Chelly.

What had seemed like five miles last night in the wind, cold and dark, turned out to be only a mile or so back to Junction Rock. I found the place where Ruby had stood off the Navajo – empty 44.40 cartridges under a little overhang of the big rock, and horse tracks in the sand where the snow didn't reach. But there wasn't any way at all to tell which way he'd gone from there, because his horse tracks got mixed up right away with others, and there wasn't any way to tell which was which.

I swung my horse and kicked his ribs and pointed him to the left of where the cliff jutted out that separated Canyon de Chelly from Canyon del Muerto. Just then, three horses came around the bulge, the same way I'd come, and their ears were up and their tails sticking out as they ran. Something back in the direction of White House Ruin had spooked them. I cut back and kicked my horse into a gallop and went back behind Junction Rock.

In about five minutes, Ruby came riding round the bend. He had his hat jammed down over his ears, a sheepskin coat turned up around his neck, and was carrying his carbine in both hands, riding slow and careful and looking all around. So he *had* spent the night somewhere up Canyon de Chelly.

I eased back the hammer on my Winchester, and let him get well out into the open . . . but not too far because I didn't want him to get past me and make a run for it out of the canyon toward Chinle.

Then my horse whinnied before he was close enough. I hollered, "Hold it right there, Ruby!" and like a flash he stood up in his stirrups and shot at me. His horse jumped sideways and mine went straight up. It was a damn good shot, because the slug went singing off Junction Rock not three feet above me. I almost came unstuck from the saddle, and by the time I got my horse lined out, Ruby had swung around and was spurring like hell back up Canyon de Chelly.

I shot at him twice, but I didn't even come close, with both of us bouncing in the saddle. So I didn't waste any more shots, but took out after him. He kept his face hung over his shoulder, and kept gigging the horse. I had him boxed now, and it didn't matter a lot if I didn't catch him right away, because I was sure going to, sooner or later.

It turned out I had the best horse, or his

had been rode harder yesterday, because I began to gain on him.

He surprised me, then. He hauled up, and threw his carbine away. He still had his six-gun, though, and I stopped fifty yards away and laid my sights on him.

I said, "Get rid of the Colt's!" At that distance, I had him cold, and he picked the six-gun out of the holster with his left hand, real careful, so I'd know he wasn't trying anything. He tossed it away, and I said, "Step down and move away from the horse."

He did, and he was grinning. He said, "Well, I did a lot of running for nothing, yesterday, didn't I!"

I didn't answer, but got down and walked over near him, with the carbine pointing at his belly.

He said, "Jesus, I damn near froze last night, till I got a fire going. And since daylight I've been trying to find a way out of here. There isn't any. So I thought I'd go back out the head of the canyon, maybe wait till dark up near Chinle, and get past. Oh, well . . ."

"Take off my money belt and toss it over here."

"You don't think I'd keep it on me!" he said, and went to laughing. "I'm gonna keep it, Link. Can't pass up six thousand dollars, can I?"

"Lay down on your belly, Ruby."

He went on talking, though. "I put it where you'll never find it. Sure, I know I'll do a year or two in Yuma for robbing you ... but six thousand, that's damn good wages for a year or two. Or maybe I know a sharp lawyer that'll get me off, for half. No, I just do my time, and come back here and pick it up after everybody's forgot about me."

He crossed his arms and put his hands up his sleeves to warm them up, or maybe to show me he wasn't going to try anything funny. "Or maybe we can deal. We both leave our guns, and I take you to where it's hid, and we split it right down the middle. How's that strike you? Half of it's a whole lot better than nothing, huh, Link?"

As if I'd trust him, without a gun to back me up!

"You're going to hand it all over, or you'll sure wish you did. And then you're going to Yuma, all right, but you ain't coming out, Ruby. Not convicted of murder, you ain't."

"You talk more foolishment than anybody I ever ..." he said, then he broke off. "What you talking about?"

"Where you got the horse," I said. "The

166

old man's dead. And the squaw and the kid saw you, and I was right on your tail. You're a gone goose, Ruby."

"Now, hold on a minute, Link."

"Get down on your belly."

He didn't, and I turned the carbine around and held it like a baseball bat and went for him. I wasn't fooling, and he knew it. He flopped down on his belly.

I laid my carbine down and took my six gun, and put my foot on the back of his head and hauled his shirt tail out of his pants. He wasn't wearing any money belt, and I went through his pockets. He didn't have any money on him at all, except a few dollars. I stepped back and said, "On your feet!"

When he was on his hands and knees, getting up, I booted him in the ass as hard as I could, and he went onto his face in the sand.

I let him get up then, and said, "We'll get mounted, and you're going to take me to where you hid it."

I stooped over to pick up his pistol, and before I could straighten up, he shot me in the ribs with a little hide-out derringer he had in his left sleeve.

It was like he'd hit me with the butt of an ax, and I was down on my face – not much hurt, yet – but I couldn't get my breath.

Then it hurt. Worst I ever felt, tearing and gouging at my left side. I was squirming and rolling on the ground and trying to yell, but I couldn't get a sound out. He looked hazy and wobbly when he walked up to me and pointed that little over-and-under derringer at my head and pulled the trigger again. The hammer clicked on the other barrel, but it was a misfire.

I got to my knees and tried to reach my Colt's where I'd dropped it ... but I just couldn't stretch my arms out, with my side one awful ache and my guts on fire and my muscles all knotted up.

He walked over and picked up his own pistol, and stood laughing at me there on my knees, hugging myself and gasping for breath. Then he took a long, deliberate aim at my head. Somewhere way behind me a rifle fired and a spout of sand flew up ten feet back of Ruby.

He jumped about three feet straight up, and ran for his horse. It shied away, but he caught the reins and got on. Then he looked back along the canyon for a minute, and turned back and aimed at my head.

I knew I ought to jump sideways or get up and run, but it was like I was frozen, paralyzed by the pain.

Then there was a flash of lightning inside

my head, without any thunder, at least I didn't hear any. I was dead.

CHAPTER 10

I was dead ... but I came back to life with my head in Mary Wilson's lap. My head felt the size of a barrel, swelling up and getting smaller, like somebody hit it with a single-jack every time it got big. She was pushing a spoon into my mouth and saying, "Come on, baby, open up for Mama, and don't spit it down my front this time."

Her face looked fuzzy, and got bigger and then smaller like my head, then faded away. I yelled when she moved and laid my head down on the sheepskin. My head felt like it exploded, and it was like somebody shoved a red hot branding iron into my left ribs and held it there. Then I could feel her hand smoothing out my forehead, and that put me to sleep.

When I woke up, I moved. That branding iron stamped me on the ribs, and I yelled again. When it cooled off a little, I was careful not to move, but I opened my eyes, and couldn't figure out where I was. I was looking up at some poles with forked ends coming together like the spokes of a wheel. A yellow light was flickering over them, and I finally figured out I was looking up at the ceiling of a hogan.

I was sweating, and I put my hand under the blankets to feel of my hurt side, and I was naked as a jaybird, except for a thick bandage. Altogether I felt like I'd been run through an ore crusher, my head wasn't swelling up any more, it just hurt like hell. There was a bandage around it, too.

I felt a rush of cold air, and Mary came in with an armful of firewood. She dumped it down with a crash that made my head hurt. I tried to sit up, and a streak of fire ran across my ribs and I couldn't get my breath. I knew where I was, and what had happened.

She got down on her knees and put her hand on my forehead and said, "Good. You're not burning up any more. You've got a broken rib. I don't know about your head."

The only reason I wasn't really dead, I guess, was that Ruby's shot at my head had plowed a furrow in my skull. It'd given me a hell of a wallop, but hadn't hit square. Mary said there was a big gouge over my left ear, and that she had dug the derringer slug out from just under a rib on my left side. Those short, rimfire .41 cartridges weren't very powerful, and my rib had stopped it from going into my heart or a lung.

Ruby would be thinking he had killed me, though.

Mary set the stew kettle beside me and spooned mutton broth into my mouth. She tried to feed me the meat, but I couldn't swallow it.

Then I had to go. I was ashamed and didn't know what to say, but she knew what was bothering me ... I guess because I looked so worried.

She said, "Let's get your boots on." She managed to put them on my bare feet without hurting me too much. But when I went to stand up and tried to keep the blanket around me at the same time, the pain hit me, and I hollered and dropped the blanket. She picked it up and wrapped it around me.

She giggled and said, "You ashamed because you've got no clothes on? You shouldn't be, after the last three days."

She got her arm around me and took my weight and picked up the lantern, and we staggered to the door. Then it hit me, what she said. "You mean it was three days ago?"

"Yes. I had to undress you and clean you up, and dig that bullet out of you and bandage you, and do everything for you. Maybe pretty soon you'll be able to go outside by yourself."

"If it kills me!" I said. My face must have been fire red, it felt that way. "You go on back," I told her. "I'll make it."

"You're not strong enough yet." Somehow she got me outside, and I was surprised to see it was dark, and there was eight inches of snow. She had tramped a path out behind the sweat hogan, and that's where she left me, and then came back when I yelled for her, and got me inside again and down on the sheepskins.

"When you left that morning," she said, "I watched you go across and look around under the White House, and then head down toward Junction Rock. And I got a funny feeling that you were going to run into trouble. I just felt like I had to hurry! And I got my gun and didn't take time to saddle up, just jumped on my horse bareback and rode after you. And before I came around the bend, I heard the shooting.

172

"Then I heard another shot, and I came around the bend and saw you on your hands and knees and him pointing that little pistol at your head. And it didn't go off, I guess, because he picked the other pistol up. I got off my horse, knelt down, and shot at him. But I didn't hit him, and while I was reloading, he caught his horse and got on. Then he shot at you and rode away down the canyon. I don't think he could see me very well, with me kneeling down that way. Maybe he thought those Navajos were after him again, like the day before.

"You were lying there on your face and blood all over you, and I couldn't get you across my horse. So I came back and hitched up the wagon and went back. I couldn't lift you, so I had to back the wagon up to a cutbank and drag you into it. And I had a bad time getting you into the hogan, because when I pulled you out of the wagon I couldn't hold you up, and you fell on the ground. You started bleeding worse, then, and I got you inside."

"Well," I said, "maybe some day I'll find some way to thank you. And now you're stuck with me."

"Oh, you'll be able to ride pretty soon if we don't get a lot more snow. I caught your horse."

173

She went out and came back with my shirt and socks and Levi's and long johns, all washed and clean, and frozen stiff as a board.

She got dinner – stewed tomatoes, fried bread, coffee, and a can of peaches for dessert. I was starving, and I ate everything she'd give me.

After she cleaned up the pots and bowls, she started to tell me something about the afternoon after Ruby shot me, something about him and some Navajos, but I couldn't stay awake. I remember seeing her make her bed the other side of the fire, and lay down with all her clothes on and pull the blankets over her . . . and that's all.

When I woke up it was daylight, and she was cooking again. When I managed to get up without losing the blanket and started to go out, she got up to help me, but I said, "I'll make it." I had to grab a roof pole till the dizziness went away. Outside, it was snowing again. I fell face down, and had a hell of a time getting up, but I sure wasn't going to have her coming with me on those little trips, any more. When I came back, she saw I was shivering and the blanket was wet. She said, "You don't have to be a damn fool."

I ached all over like I'd been run over by a herd of buffalo, but I was able to sit up propped against the wall, and have my

174

breakfast. She had already fed and watered the horses and sheep, and brought firewood in from the stack by the corral.

I asked her, "What was that you were saying about Ruby and some Navajos, that afternoon after he shot me?"

"He got away, out of the canyon. I got you back here before noon, and then pretty soon I heard shooting down by Junction Rock again, and coming closer. I got scared, and called the dogs. I got my gun, and climbed up the side of the canyon a little ways till I found a place behind some rocks where I could see out over the trees. I thought maybe somebody knew about my hogan and would try to hide in here, and I was afraid to stay inside.

"And Ruby – I was pretty sure it had to be him – he came up the canyon on a horse, looking back over his shoulder, and behind him there were ten or eleven Navajos. They were all shooting at him, and he went down. I mean his horse went down, turned clear over, and he laid there on the sand. I thought he was dead. But he got up, got his gun, and ran, and started to climb up to White House Ruin. When he got into the trees at the bottom of the slope, the Navajos stopped. Then he shot from the door of the ruin, and they scattered out. Some went into the trees under White

House Ruin and tied their horses, and some hid on this side.

"They were shooting all afternoon, but he was inside the ruin and they couldn't hit him. He didn't shoot very much, sometimes from the door and sometimes from up on the roof. I don't think he hit anybody. For a long time, nobody shot, because they couldn't see him. Then when he'd shoot, all the Navajos shot back. Then somebody shot from up above where I was hiding ... some Navajo up on the trail that starts up on this side, near here, maybe so Ruby wouldn't get away up there. It started to get dark. Then I saw Ruby on the roof, and that Navajo up on the trail took another shot and almost hit him. I saw dust fly and a couple of stones fell out of the edge of the roof, right where he was.

"Ruby raised up then, and all the Navajos in the trees on both sides of the canyon were shooting at him, but he didn't pay any attention to them. He aimed a long time, and shot, and the Navajo up on the trail yelled and fell down the cliff. He bounced off the rocks, turned over, and fell into the trees the other side of my corral."

"So that showed Ruby there was a trail up the cliff," I said.

"I guess so," she said. "The Navajos started to leave, then. They got their horses where they had them tied, sneaked out through the trees, and rode away. I guess they got scared when he shot that one. And they were scared of the dark. They don't want to be down here when the ghosts and witches come out.

"Soon as they were gone, Ruby came down out of the White House, walked across, and started looking for the trail. Well, he found it, and went up right past me. I was scared, because my dogs were growling and I was trying to hold their mouths shut. He heard it and looked around, but he didn't see me and didn't stop."

I said, "I guess they were watching for him up at the end of the canyon, that morning he shot me. They must have sent somebody around the rim to guard the top of the trail, too. Well, there goes my sixty-three hundred dollars."

"You mean he took it?" she said. "You told me he didn't have it. And he sure didn't go get it, that day."

"No, he didn't have it on him. It's hid somewhere in the canyon. But I haven't got him, either, to make him tell where it is. Maybe they still caught him. He didn't have a horse, and they could run him down the next day."

"Maybe," she said. "But they sure wouldn't chase him at night. And he killed one of them. They wouldn't be in a hurry to get close to him again."

"What did they do about the dead one?"

"Nothing. Just left him. They weren't going to touch any dead man."

"But maybe he was only hurt. Didn't you go and see?"

She said. "You go look! Not me!"

She was as scared of a dead man as any full-blooded Navajo. Of course, he'd be dead by now, even if he wasn't when Ruby shot him.

"Well, I'll be in shape to ride before long. I'll find out if anybody saw Ruby, or if he got to the railroad."

"You're not going to ride for quite a while."

"Well, then, somebody'll come looking for me. Beasley or somebody, and take me out in a wagon. Or you can take me out."

"If it keeps on snowing, nobody's going to come down here or go out, either, for a long time. And who's going to come for you? Beasley got hit on the head, and he's a sick man. I know that. And those Navajos, they don't give a damn about you or any white man. What do they care if you're dead or alive? And Sam Day, why I bet you that Navajo that works for him didn't even tell him about your coming through Chinle. That's white man's business, and Navajos just

178

don't care. And even if he or Beasley know, they can't get down here at all. This place is clear out of the world all winter."

"Well, you're down here," I said. "What about that? Or were you going to leave, and then couldn't because you're stuck with me?"

"No. I stay down here. I don't go out in winter."

I asked her how come, and she shut up and wouldn't talk any more. In fact, for about a week she wouldn't talk any more than she had to, except when she was mad at me. On one of my trips out behind the sweat hogan, I tried to bring back an armful of wood, just to help out and show her I appreciated all she was doing for me. But my head began to spin and I fell down. She had to drag me back inside, and my wound broke open again and was bleeding. She was mad enough to slug me. She yammered at me like any wife would. She wanted to help me on my little trips outside again, but I wouldn't let her do that if it killed me, and that made her even madder. It was four more days before I could get out of the blankets except when I absolutely had to. I could do a few little things for her, though, like grinding the Arbuckle's in her old coffee mill, and keeping the fire going when she was tending the horses and getting in the wood.

One thing I was real glad of. She had

found my carbine where Ruby shot me. He had picked up his own carbine, but I guess an extra one wasn't any use to him. I cleaned the carbine, and cleaned up Mary's old Remington rolling block carbine the best I could. It was a mess, the barrel so foul you could hardly see through it, and the stock split and wrapped with rawhide. She had eight old .50 caliber rimfire shells for it, the copper green as grass.

It kept snowing, off and on, and not melting at all now and I finally got used to the idea that I was going to be here a long time. Most likely I'd never catch up with Ruby Blair in my life . . . but I wasn't anxious any more, or itching to get going. It was pretty wonderful down there in the tight, warm hogan . . . almost like being married. Except that even when I got so I could get dressed in the morning and move around pretty good, there wasn't anything between Mary and me at all. Maybe if she had let on she wanted to get friendly, but she never did, not even by a look on her face or anything. You'd think that living together there in that sixteen-foot-diameter hogan twenty-four hours a day, that something would have happened. But she never took her clothes off, at least inside the hogan. She slept in them, like all the Navajo women. But every few days she'd change her clothes outside, and it must have damn near froze her. One time she built a fire in the sweat hogan, and took a bath. When she came in she was wrapped in a blanket, and she told me she'd kill me if I looked while she put on her clothes. I didn't try to look, but laid on my sheepskins with my back turned till she said, "All right."

That was after she had killed another sheep, because we were running out of meat. It wasn't snowing that day, and I went out to help if I could. Well, she sure didn't need any help from me! I'd dressed out a lot of game and beef, but nothing to compare with her. She had the head and legs off and the carcass hung up and gutted and the hide peeled in about ten minutes, and she never wasted a move.

We'd lay there on opposite sides of the fire at night, with the light flickering on the roof, warm and cozy, and us full of good mutton, fried bread, canned peaches and coffee. She began to loosen up a little ... asking me questions about what I'd done all my life, where I'd been, and if I was married and things like that.

And for quite a while, I never saw so much as her bare ankle, or heard one thing unladylike from her. I laughed to myself when I thought how I used to think Callie was a lady. This Mary Wilson – Adezhbah –

was a real lady, and a very good looking one.

It would have been easy to think I was falling in love with her, but I didn't try to fool myself or her, either. But I sure liked her, everything about her, and I respected her, too. She made it plain enough that she didn't want any funny business, and even if I'd felt like it, I wouldn't have tried anything, because there wasn't any place she could have run to or anyone to help her if I'd tried to get rough. I guess the real reason, though, was that I wasn't well yet, not by a long shot.

I couldn't figure, though, why she was living alone, and why she stayed by herself down here in the canyon. Navajos like to be together. That is, most of them don't gather in towns or villages, but the families are real close. There'll be four or five hogans way the hell away from anywhere, and everybody related . . . the sisters' husbands and kids all there. When they get married, the husband goes to live with his wife's family instead of setting up his own place, among his own clan.

Anyway, when I asked her, she said, "My people aren't friends with me, and I've got no relatives except my mother's clan, and they don't like me, either, because I went to school."

"A lot of Navajos been to school," I said. "Franklin Yazzie, and Hosteen Lichee's boy, and his uncle and a lot of others."

"Not to college," she said. "After I got through at Tuba City, I went to the Sherman Institute, over in Riverside, California. My father sent me. He said I was going to be educated, so I wouldn't have to spend my life tending sheep and living in a dirty hogan where I'd go blind from smoke, and spend six weeks weaving a rug to sell to some trader for six dollars." She kind of grinned, but not like it was funny. "So here I am living in a smokey hogan, anyway."

"Old Man Beasley told me about it," I said. "And about how your mother and father got drowned. I'm sure sorry, Mary."

After that, she wouldn't say any more.

I lost track of time. I'd look across at the north wall of the canyon, with White House Ruin tucked in that cave in the tremendous cliff, and not a mark on the snow, nothing moving, and not a sound ... just a lost world with only the two of us. I'd lie awake, daydreaming at night, thinking how I used to want to live on the reservation and get away from people like Harry Peters, and towns, and noise and maybe responsibility, too, if I'm going to be honest ... and now here I had it, everything I used to dream about. Only it wasn't Callie in this daydream, not any more. And I almost didn't regret what happened. I was just plain lucky I found out about Callie before it was too late. And if it hadn't been for losing the money, and the way I lost it, I'd never have known how wonderful this kind of life could be ... even with a busted rib and a shot-up head. And now, they were better every day. And the better they got, the harder it got to stay there. Because Mary was pretty used to me, now, and she was getting a little careless about keeping herself covered up every minute, and about touching me, or brushing against me. I'm pretty sure – but actually, I really don't know – that she didn't mean anything by it, that she wasn't trying to tease me or get me stirred up. But maybe she was, maybe even without realizing it. Because, she was young and healthy, and she had to have the same kind of instincts I did. I was sure tempted to find out, but I didn't dare risk it, for fear I was seeing something that wasn't there, and all I would do would be scare the hell out of her, or make her mad.

I don't know how many more days went by before she loosened up and told me about herself.

"I liked going to college," she said. "All kinds of Indians were there, Apaches, Papagos, Hualapais, Mojaves, and Plains Indians from Oklahoma. They taught us how to cook and make clothes, and in the last two years how to make a living off the reservation. I bet you never saw another Indian girl that could take shorthand and write a business letter. But I was homesick, too. I missed my mother and father and my friends around the Ram House Trading Post where I grew up. I even thought maybe I could be a teacher and come back and help my people, but it didn't work out. When I graduated, I tried to get a job in Phoenix, and nobody would hire me. I wanted to live like a white girl, then, and maybe get married and raise a family, but I was a dirty blanket Indian to those white people. Then one of my teachers got me a job in a rich man's home. I helped in the kitchen, served the dinner, and cleaned house. The woman was good to me, but every time she was out of the house, the man was chasing me around, trying to get me to bed. Well, I laid his head open with a frying pan one time, and they put me in jail. My father came down and got me out, and brought me home, then, back to our cabin by the Ram House Trading Post. I never left the reservation again.

"But I made a bad mistake. I tried to help my old girl friends, you know, show them how to keep clean, make clothes and help themselves, and they didn't like it. All they could talk about was boys, sheep, weaving rugs, getting married, and going to the Sings and Squaw Dances. Well, I liked that part of it, too, but when I'd go, none of the boys would dance with me even when I paid them, the way the girl has to do at a Squaw Dance. At least, they wouldn't with the old long-hairs looking on. They were after me enough when they could get me alone, though. So then, after my father and mother got drowned, I moved down here into Canyon de Chelly. My father had this hogan built because he loved the canyon, and we always moved down here as soon as we could in the spring, and stayed till winter."

I was feeling good enough to help out some, now. If I took it easy and didn't try too much on any one day, I could get in some wood, or go down and break the ice in the creek and fill the water barrel, or bring in cottonwood bark, for the horses. That's all they ate after the hay was gone, but they liked it.

I was so much better she really began to bother me. It got so it was awful hard to keep my hands off her. She'd put her hand on my arm sometimes when she talked to me, and she'd laugh up into my face, with her black eyes crinkled up. And she got real careless about keeping her legs covered up when she got onto her sheepskins at night, across the fire, and pulled the blankets over her. And a couple of times when it was real hot in the hogan, and she'd be sewing or something, she'd pull all those skirts up above her knees. Or maybe she'd just turn her back instead of going outside, when she pulled off her blouse to change it, or so it wouldn't get wet when she washed her hair. And of course, even if I couldn't see what was on the front of her chest, I could sure imagine them as plain as day. And a couple of times, I had to get up and go out and tramp around in the snow to cool down. And when I came back, she just grinned at me, and didn't ask me why I went out.

But I couldn't forget all she was doing for me, and I was pretty sure she didn't really want me to start anything. I was pretty sure, too, that she didn't have any idea how hard it was for me. Maybe it's easier for women to hold off, I don't know.

One day she got a picture out from behind a blanket hung on the wall. It was wrapped up in another blanket, and she took it off very carefully. It was a painting of a woman, a very pretty young Navajo woman loaded with jewelry and smiling at you like she was about to talk to you.

"This is my mother," Mary said. "My father painted it." And I saw it was signed "Ellsworth Wilson," like the painting of Old Man Beasley.

"Beasley told me about him," I said. "He must have been a wonderful man. And I never saw anything like that! Why, she's as pretty as you!"

She said, "Well, he never saw any place he liked as much as the reservation, and he liked Navajo people, and painted a lot of pictures just because he wanted to, besides the ones for the railroad. He had a big exhibition in New York, and most of them sold. He got as much as a thousand dollars for one picture, and there's one now in the Metropolitan Museum, and in the Smithsonian Institute."

She began to wrap up the painting, but I said, "Let me look at it some more."

She went on, "Well, he never went back. He said he belonged out here. Then he painted this picture of my mother, and after while he married her. They really loved each other. When I was born, they moved to Flagstaff, because he wanted to bring me up in a city where I could go to school with the white kids. But they called him a squaw man and said bad things to my mother, and nobody would visit them at their house except people who knew the Navajos, like the Babbitt family. So we came back to the reservation, and he said he was never going back. He built the cabin near the trading post, and this hogan."

She took the picture, wrapped it up, and put it back.

"He left me quite a lot of money," she said. "Old Man Beasley, he was like a father to me, after that, and told me how to take care of my money, and talked to tourists and museum people that wanted to buy the paintings that were left. He bargained with them and got good prices, and never took one penny for it."

She sat down beside me again, and I took hold of her hand and said, "I guess it's been a pretty lonesome life for you. That ain't right. I wish I could . . ."

"Oh," she said, "I was lonesome at first. But I'm Navajo, Link, and I love my people and my land. I'm not even a Christian. I go to the Sings and listen to the chants, and I believe in First Man and First Woman, and how my people came here. I wouldn't be white if I could. I have a good life, and I don't want anything else."

She seemed to realize I was holding her hand, then, and pulled it away. She said, "Sometimes I almost think my father was a Navajo with blue eyes. He knew more Sings and chants than some of the medicine men, and he knew all about the Anasazi Old People and the ruins. Why, he even gave me my Navajo name. It was my mother that named me Mary."

"Adezhbah," I said. "That's a pretty name. What's it mean?"

"It means 'Little Warrior Girl'. Most Navajo girls get war names when they're little," she said. "I could tell you why but it wouldn't make any sense to you. But my father knew."

Well, I'd been lonesome, plenty of times, but never like she must have been. I wanted to say something or do something to tell her I was sorry and knew how she felt . . . tell her I thought she was beautiful, or that I liked her better than anyone I'd ever known, and I reached for her hand again. She pulled it away and got up in a hurry to mix some dough for fried bread.

I wondered how these long weeks would have been if I'd been Navajo or she'd been all white, and I almost wished it was that way. But I sure didn't want to turn squaw man, even though I thought a man could sure do worse than tie up with Mary.

The time didn't go slow by any means. She felt easy with me by now, and we talked about everything under the sun. I told her why I had tried to buy the Ram House Trading Post, and how the country had really got under my skin. She said she always traded at the Ram House Trading Post instead of with Sam Day at Chinle, which was right next door, you

190

might say, because Old Man Beasley had been so good to her after her folks were drowned.

I tried to keep from thinking how it would have been if Ruby hadn't stolen my money. I'd have owned the post by now, probably, and my dream would have come true. Another thought began to bother me, and I tried to keep it out of my mind ... the kind of life it would be, with Mary there with me instead of Callie, the way I used to dream. Hard as I tried, I couldn't keep from daydreaming about it and the more I did, the more I knew it would have been wonderful.

I'd given up thinking somebody would come and get me out. Maybe Sam Day had tried and couldn't make it. Nobody back in Prescott would know where I was, or care about it, either. Old Man Beasley might have heard about me and the Navajos coming down into the canyon after Ruby, and me not coming out, but he sure didn't know I was shot. Maybe the Navajos had got Ruby. And I wondered about Callie. If Ruby got away, maybe she had been in touch with him, and I could find her and make her tell me where he was.

Maybe it was because I'd been sick and had just let myself drift and enjoy being with Mary, like it was a world of our own, and hadn't thought about what I'd do when it came to an end. But now I got restless and began to worry, which I hadn't done since the day Ruby shot me. It really hit me now, my stake gone, not a cent to my name. I couldn't go back to Prescott, not and be laughed at, and run into trouble with Harry Peters. I'd had all the trouble I wanted, and nothing to gain from looking for more. I'd have to go back to the only thing I knew how to do – ride fence, grease windmills, rope calves, and comb the hills at roundup time. Forty a month and my grub. It made me sick inside.

I was well now, and I couldn't for the life of me figure what date it was. Mary didn't care about that. Time didn't mean a thing to her, the way it does to a white man. But she said it was February, and I could hardly believe it.

CHAPTER 11

It hadn't snowed for about two weeks, and one night I woke up and heard water dripping. Next day the sun was out strong, and the snow got mushy. When I went to the creek for water, I could hear it running under the ice.

That afternoon, I began to look my gear over, what there was of it, the carbine, saddle, and saddlebags. The saddle could have stood a good soaping, but all Mary had was mutton fat, and I couldn't use that.

She said, "Looks like you're getting ready to travel."

"Well, I have to soon as I can. Might as well be ready."

"You'll still be here a while."

It froze again, hard, that night, and for three or four days it didn't get above freezing. It was an aggravation, because I was real restless, now, wanting to get going. I had decided I'd make a hard try to find Ruby. I'd find out if the Navajos had got him or knew anything about where he'd gone, and I'd check the railroad stations at Gallup, Winslow, and Flagstaff to see if anyone remembered him getting on a train. If I couldn't get any lead on him, I'd find Callie and see what she knew. Only if I couldn't find any lead at all, then I'd find a job.

But that wasn't the only reason I got restless. Animals do, in the spring, and men, I guess, all the time – if they haven't got any holes in their head and ribs, and there's a good looking woman around. It was all I could do, now, to keep my hands off Mary. She must have known it . . . she didn't have to be told a lot of things, she just knew, without having to depend on her eyes and ears. But I wouldn't hurt her or scare her or make her think she couldn't trust me any more, for anything in the world. I knew I had to get out. I didn't have any idea what she really thought of me, even after all those weeks. She'd saved my life, cared for me like a baby, and fed me, but whether I meant anything at all to her I just didn't know. The Navajo half of her most likely didn't trust any white man except Old Man Beasley. I was tempted to try and find out.

Then the cottonwoods began to show green. You could hardly see it, you just kind of felt it, at first, before the buds really popped out. Then it thawed, overnight, and everything was dripping, and the creek ran like a mill race. It spread out and sluiced the snow away. We were stuck in the hogan for four days. Even the air was wet, and the hogan full of smoke. The third morning when I looked out, the creek spread from wall to wall across the canyon and came almost up to the hogan. Mary began to talk about driving out to the Ram House Trading Post for supplies. She told me she guessed I'd be glad to go, and it wouldn't be but a day or two. That's when I thought she might tell me she'd miss me, and that all this time together meant something to her. But she didn't.

I said, "Before I go, I'm going to have a

look for my money. Ruby left it somewhere up the canyon, that's sure."

"There's a thousand places. You'll waste your time."

"What places?"

"Well, the hogans. He had to stay some place that night where he could get out of the cold and have a fire."

"I'll look into them."

"It might be buried under a fire pit, or stuck on top of a rafter pole," she said. "It would take you months to look every place, and the Navajos will be coming back as soon as they can get their wagons in, so you can't search all the hogans."

I said, "He was in a hell of a hurry that day. He wouldn't have had time to pick a special place. And it was already getting dark when he stood off the Navajos at Junction Rock. He had to hide it after that. He must've left it where he spent the night. Now if I was to ride up the canyon from Junction Rock, and put myself in his place . . . why maybe it would strike me the way it did him. Maybe I'd spot the same place he did. If I go at it that way, and take a look in every place he might have spotted, I might just find it."

"It could be in a ruin," she said. "And it would have to be one near the bottom of the canyon, because he couldn't have climbed up to one of the high ones if it was too dark. There's a lot of them. Why don't you try the White House? That's the first one he'd come to."

I tried the White House that same day. I plowed through the water – it wasn't more than ankle deep anywhere – and climbed up to the building, looking till dark. Some of the rooms were dry as a bone, with pack rat tracks all over the floor, and *manos, metates,* and a lot of broken pots. Some big ones that weren't broken still had corncobs and seed shells in them after a thousand years. But I couldn't even check all the obvious places, like the tops of *vigas,* and places in the walls where stones and plaster had fallen out. It would take a year. And there weren't any boot tracks. I was feeling real low when I waded back to the hogan after sundown. It would take an army to search every ruin in the canyon, and still that money belt might be tucked away in some little hole, or buried, and they'd never find it.

When I came back, I was soaked and my feet were numb, and I sat by the fire and dried out.

Mary said, "There's other ruins he would have seen, depending on how far up the canyon he went that first night. The next one, about a mile past the White House,

196

wouldn't be easy to get into, though. It's as close to the bottom of the canyon, but it's on top of a high wall above a real steep slope. It's built out of special red stones, so they call it Red Ruin. Then there's a little one right at the bottom of the cliff, with a big white cow painted beside it on the cliff wall. And then, Antelope House, with painted antelopes on the cliff above. They wouldn't be hard to get into."

I knew it was hopeless, but I couldn't give up and say I was beat. I wouldn't go back to working on a ranch, not till I tried the best I could,

After the big run-off, the creek settled back into its channel, or rather channels. I thought the canyon floor would be a slough of mud, but the sand dried out and drained off within a day after the flood stopped. You could walk on it better than when it was real dry. That was three days after I hunted through White House Ruin, and that afternoon I told Mary I was going to give it one more try. I'd go into those other ruins she told me about, or any other likely looking ones I saw when I rode up the canyon.

When I went out to get some firewood, the bare cottonwoods and a piñon pine over the wood pile were still dripping from last night's rain. I got my shirt wet and when I came in and dumped down the firewood, I took it off, and hung it on a nail in a rafter. I stripped off the upper part of my long johns, too.

I was standing by the fire, drying off, and I said, "I thought of something. The rooms in White House Ruin were dry, with a layer of dust an inch thick. You could see animal tracks all over – pack rats and ground squirrels. Now if he did stay in a ruin that night, there'll sure be some sign ... foot tracks or a recent fire. I know it's hopeless to try to check over all the hogans, but if he took shelter in a ruin and I can find the right one, I'll know he's been there. You want to help me look?"

She got a funny look on her face, and said, "No, I'll stay here."

I laughed at her and said, "You scared of those ruins?"

"They're *chindee!* Those Old People, the Anasazi, sometimes they're still there! And there's dead ones, mummies, buried under the floors and in the old Basket Maker storage bins."

She was scared, and I changed the subject, and didn't laugh at her any more. I put my arm around her shoulders. She tried to pull away, but I held her. I said, just joking – or maybe I was serious, I don't know – "Well, I'll find the money tomorrow, and go and buy the post from Old Man Beasley. Only I'm gonna need a helper that talks Navajo, till I can learn. Maybe some pretty little squaw. You know one would do? Maybe somebody named Adezhbah?"

She stepped square in front of me and snarled, "You dirty, Belecana white-eyes! You think you can insult me and make fun of me just because I'm Indian?"

She swung her right arm full length and hit me in the face as hard as she could. She started to hit me again, and I reached around her, grabbed her wrist, and bent her arm up behind her back. Then she tried to hit me with her left hand, and I grabbed that one the same way. She sure had a chip on her shoulder about white men, and about being Indian. I didn't mean anything wrong, and she didn't have any call to hit me. I was as mad as she was.

She was swearing and spitting like a trapped bobcat, and she bit me on the shoulder. I hollered, and got my shoulder under her chin and bent her backward. She was twisting and squirming, trying to wrench loose, and her blouse got pushed up so her warm, bare belly was against me. All that sure didn't cool me down any!

She was strong as a bobcat, too, and she shoved me off balance. I stuck my foot in the

199

edge of the fire, and knocked the stew kettle over. We slammed into the wall, knocked over a stack of coffee crates full of canned goods, and tripped, landing with me on my back and her on top, kicking and struggling and jerking at my hands. I hung on, and kept her hands pinned behind her. I gave a big heave, and rolled over on top of her, all tangled up in blanket and sheepskins.

She whispered, "I'll kill you! I'll kill you!" and she was using all her strength and every trick she could think of to break my grip. I hung on and rode my weight on her. By now her blouse was half torn and her skirts wadded up around her hips. I wasn't worrying any more about scaring her or hurting her feelings . . . no matter what I did, I couldn't possibly make her any madder.

I shoved my knee in between her legs and put my mouth on hers, and she twisted her head from side to side trying to keep me from kissing her.

I was beyond the point of thinking, now. I was going to have her, and nothing could stop me. Only I couldn't figure out how to let go of her hands and still hold her down so I could get the clothes off her.

She was saying something, but there was a roaring in my ears, and my heart was hammering against her bare breast, and I wasn't listening to anything she said.

Then suddenly she went limp, quit struggling and jerking her hands and wrenching her head around, and she kissed me, long and hot and hard. "Wait, Link! Wait! You're breaking my arms! Let me up, just for a minute! Let me get ready!"

So I rolled off her and let her hands go. She slid to one side, propped on her left arm, and I didn't see that she was reaching out with her right hand. She got hold of the upended cast iron stew kettle by the bail and swung it, and caught me on the side of the head, right where Ruby Blair's bullet had whacked me. I saw that brilliant, silent lightning flash again inside my head, and that was all.

I don't know how long before I woke up, maybe five minutes, maybe an hour. The fire was low, and stinking with burned stew, and the hogan was a mess, with boxes, shelves, and canned goods scattered around, and clothing knocked off the hooks. My head hurt so bad it felt like it was going to break open. It was bleeding, too. I could feel it trickling down past my ear.

But none of that mattered, because Mary was sitting on that wad of blankets in her torn blouse, hugging my head to her breasts — two warm, velvety cushions — and her *chongo* knot had come loose. Her black, tangled hair was around us like a soft cloud. Her face was against mine, and wet with tears.

She was rocking me gently, and whispering, "Don't die! Oh, Link, don't die! I didn't want to hurt you!"

I didn't play fair. For a while I didn't let her know I had come to. But, my God, I couldn't stand to just lay there like a sack! And when I ran the palm of my hand up the soft inside of her thigh, she gasped and stiffened, then bent her head down and kissed me hard. Then she pushed me away, and pulled the wreck of her blouse off over her head.

In a minute, we were both naked, and she rolled onto the wadded up blankets and sheepskins and pulled me down on her. The next couple of minutes . . . or five, or ten, whatever it was . . . were wild and savage, and I'll never forget it as long as I live. Nothing to compare with it will ever happen to me again.

But I swore I would never understand her, either. We were lying there, after, hugged tight together, the whole brown sweet length of her against me, and me half dazed and half asleep . . . and all of a sudden she pushed away, got up, and threw her clothes on any old way. She stood there with her back to me, and bent her head and put her face in her hands for a while, then said, very calm and quiet, "Go sleep in the wagon."

Well, I blustered and argued, asked questions and demanded an answer, and finally I got mad and swore at her, and she just stood there. I got my bedding and went out.

I found the wagon cover wrapped in a tarp along with the harness, under the wagon seat. I spread the tarp in the wagon box and made my bed there. I was comfortable enough, but I couldn't get to sleep. I thought, Why the hell did she have to take it that way? Can't she see it had to happen, her and me together all this time? And what's so bad about it? Why should it bother her like that? Hell, no harm done, is there?

I was mad, and still puzzled, but I was sorry for her, too – neither white nor Navajo like that, and both sides turning her away, and having to live by herself like a hermit down in the bottom of a canyon, and never have a good friend she could be free with and laugh with . . . not even any kin of her own anywhere.

I rolled over and pulled the blankets up around my ears and thought. Well, there's nothing I can do. But I still kept thinking about her. This would be my last night here, and I'd have to go away and never see her again, or know how she was doing.

I knew I'd never forget her. I was even sorry, now, that it had happened, because it had spoiled everything between us. I felt sad, and I thought I'd get up and knock on the door and ask her if I couldn't come in and sleep this one more time across the fire from her.

I wanted to, real bad, but I didn't want another slap in the face – didn't want it to be any worse than it was already.

Then I heard the hogan door creak, and she called out, real soft, "Link?"

I said, "I'm awake, Mary."

She came and climbed in over the tailgate, and I lifted the corner of the tarp and blankets, and she crawled in and laid beside me. She didn't touch me, just laid there stiff as a poker. I could tell how embarrassed she was, because her face and neck felt hot. For a long time, I just held her close, and she finally relaxed and put her arms around me. Then I had a hard time finding her under those four or five skirts. She had put on another blouse, and I fumbled with it and got it off her. Her hair was still undone, and it was all over my face and shoulders, soft and silky and fragrant.

We were gentle with each other.

Then she cuddled close to me with her face against mine, and neither of us said anything.

I almost told her I loved her, and I wanted to hear her say it, but I couldn't quite do it. I mean, I wouldn't lie to her, even now, and I honestly didn't know if I was in love with her. I was glad she didn't ask me but I guess she never would, not with her pride. And I began to be ashamed, because I thought she wouldn't have been there if she didn't love me, and I felt like I was cheating her.

I'm not sure whether we went to sleep or not. I didn't want to. I just wanted to lie there quiet with her in my arms. I remember thinking what a shame it was that we'd wasted all that time the last week or so, when I'd really been feeling good again. Way up on the rim somewhere, a coyote howled, lonesome and sad, and Mary's dogs told him what they thought of him.

Then as soon as the sun hit the edge of the north rim, she got up, went into the trees, then into the hogan, and built up the fire. When I came in, it was like every morning for the last two months and more. There weren't any smiles or pats on the behind, she was just matter-of-fact like always. She didn't say a word about yesterday afternoon or last night, just got breakfast and went about her business. I grabbed her once when she went past me, but she pulled away. Well, after last night, you can bet it was a big let-down to me, and I knew she was ashamed, and sorry it happened.

After breakfast, I saddled the horse and made sure the carbine had a full load, and waited around to see if she would come out. I couldn't just ride off like I'd never seen her in my life. She did come out, then, with some fried bread and a piece of cooked mutton wrapped in a flour sack. I put it in my saddlebag, and turned to say goodbye to her, and she was already walking back to the hogan.

I hurried after her, got her by the shoulders, and turned her around. She didn't fight me, just stood there looking straight into my eyes, and no expression on her face. I smiled at her, and said, "Mary . . ." and she didn't even blink. I pulled her against me and bent down to kiss her, and she turned her face away and pushed at me.

I got mad then. "What the hell is this! All night in the blankets with me, and now you won't even look at me! Listen, if it hadn't been for you, I'd be dead. I don't know how I'll ever pay you back. Do you think it doesn't mean a damn thing to me? What the hell you think happened last night? You think you got raped, or something? You figure it wasn't you came and crawled into my blankets? Maybe I broke your door down and jumped you, or something?"

She twisted, but I hung on to her. Then she relaxed and wouldn't look at me, but she said, "The only reason you're here at all is that I couldn't turn you away, not that first night when you were cold and hungry, and the next day when you were shot. That doesn't give you any claim to me. If you think last night meant anything more than just a little fun for me, you're a fool. I don't trust anybody with white skin and blue eyes. As soon as you ride around that bend, you never existed. I'll be rid of you, and can go back to living the way I want to!"

I held her chin and made her look at me, then. Her face was like it was carved out of wood . . . but when she pulled my hands loose and turned away, I saw tears in her eyes.

Well, I'd rather she'd have spit in my face or kicked my sore ribs, or swore at me for seducing her. I couldn't say anything, I could only watch her walk away. I was mad as hell, but something hurt me inside.

I said, "What if we have a kid?"

She turned around then, and put her fists on her hips and said, "Not we! Just me! Navajo babies belong to their mother. The father doesn't mean a thing! And no Navajo gives a damn if a girl has a baby without being married. And they don't give a damn if she's a virgin or not when they marry her! Just consider yourself lucky! If you slept with a white girl, she'd have you chained hand and foot for the rest of your life! Mrs. Link Conway! That's what she'd be. Well not me, thanks!"

She started to walk away from the hogan. I couldn't figure it out at all!

She looked back again, and said, "I'm going to take a look around. Maybe it was a bear or a lion that set the dogs to barking last night, and I don't want anything to happen to my sheep. You be gone when I get back!"

I got on the horse, but I couldn't quite say, "The hell with it!" and ride away. I watched her walk away. This was a hell of a way to say goodbye, after living together two months, and specially after last night.

She kept on walking, not looking back. All of a sudden she stopped, bent down, and looked at the ground. Then she straightened up, looked back, and hollered, "Link!"

I almost told her to go to hell, but I kicked the horse and rode over to her.

There was a line of footprints, boot tracks, not moccasin tracks, that came out of the cottonwoods at the bottom of the talus slope. I rode beside them, backtracking them to see where they came from, and they went in a big bend around the hogan and corral, maybe a hundred yards away, and led back to the foot of the trail that climbed out of the canyon.

Something stunk over there, a terrible, sickly sweet stink that turned my stomach. I saw the dead Navajo that had been on ice, you might say, over two months. But he was thawing out, now, and it wasn't improving him any. He was the one that had fallen off the trail when Ruby Blair shot him, and showed Ruby where the trail went up.

I rode back to Mary and looked at where the tracks went on from there. They angled across to the other side of the canyon, past the White House Ruin, and kept going out of sight around a bullnose of cliff.

CHAPTER 12

It was Ruby Blair. Besides all the reasons that came to mind, I knew it inside of me, as sure as I was sitting there on that Indian horse. The reasons were not so much that the tracks were made by high-heeled boots – some of the Navajos wore cowboy boots – but no other white man had any business down in the canyon. And no Navajo would have walked down that footpath when he could use the other trail and ride in on a horse or wagon, and no Navajo that ever lived would come down that trail in the dark, not with the *chindee* ghosts and witch coyotes running around at night.

I rode to the corral and unsaddled and turned the horse in. Mary came along. She said, "So it's him, isn't it? And after all the talk, you're not going after him?"

"I don't have to," I said. "I can just pick a place to lay for him and let him dig up the money belt and bring it to me. He has to come back this way."

"But," she said, "he can wait till dark, and . . ."

"I know it," I said. "But he won't get by me this time. There's going to be some shooting, whatever he does. I ain't interested in killing him, but he tried to kill me, and he will if he can. If I get all brave and go charging after him on a horse – a big, fat target – he'll do it for sure this time. So I'll just trail along on foot and try to keep out of sight till he's got that money belt and starts out with it. If I jump him before he digs it up and have to kill him to stay alive myself, then I'll never get my hands on it. He sure can't hide his tracks in wet sand, and I'll find him. At least, I'll know what ruin he goes into, if he really hid it in one of them, or hogan, or whatever."

"Well, goodbye," she said, and turned to go to the hogan. Not, "Good luck," or "Oh, Link, take care of yourself," or anything like that.

I said, "Shall I stop and see you when it's over, Mary? When I come back for the horse?"

She turned around and stared at me. She said, "And you'll show me a handful of money, maybe – if you don't get your head shot off – and hire me to work in your trading post and haggle in Navajo with your customers, and then when you close for the night, cook your dinner and then jump into bed with you? Maybe I'd even have time to wash your clothes, between jobs, like I did when I picked you up and brought you here. Well, thanks very much, Link!" She went into the hogan.

I just couldn't figure her out at all, so angry and bitter . . . and last night in bed with me. But I could think about that later.

I made sure I had the spare cartridges in my pocket, with one in the breech of the carbine, and the hammer on half cock, before I ducked into the trees scattered at the bottom of the cliff. I stayed on the south side and went careful, and kept watching for Ruby in the trees on the other side. Pretty soon I could see around that big bullnose of the northside cliff, where his tracks went ... and a long stretch up the canyon, maybe half a mile. He wasn't in sight. His tracks went into the trees there. I kept going and kept looking. The canyon made some twists and turns, and a couple of times I was forced to get out in the open to go around fallen rock. It was beginning to narrow, and I could see where Ruby had to do the same thing sometimes. I wanted to cross over, but there just wasn't any cover on that sand floor except a few shallow washes that wouldn't cover me and didn't go anywhere. It was touchy, because he might have backtracked just to make sure he was alone, and the hair kind of stood up on the back of my neck every time I had to expose myself. I'd gone more than a mile from the hogan and, looking back, I couldn't see it any more because of the twists of the canyon and parts of it jutting out.

When I finally saw him, I almost gave myself away. I had to look real hard across a couple hundred yards of flat sand to the trees near the cliff so I'd see his tracks when he had to get out from cover. I was afraid I'd get ahead of him. Then I had to go out in the open myself, to get around a jumble of big, fallen rocks. I watched the other side for two or three minutes, then started to walk out real slow. If I hurried, he might see movement. Then I heard rocks falling, on the other side.

I sprinted back, and made a high dive over a cottonwood log. I expected to hear his gun and see the chips fly. Nothing happened. I was staring at the trees over there, when a couple of small rocks came bouncing down a steep slope against the cliff behind the trees – a forty-five degree talus of fallen rocks and dirt. I looked up, and there was Ruby, spread-eagled on an old wall that went up from the top of the slope. I could have nailed him, blindfolded.

He was using fingers and toes to inch his way up a long crack in the wall, a retaining wall that kept the bank from caving in. These Old People knew something about engineering, you can bet. That wall was no less than forty feet high, and it had a batter – it sloped inward about three feet from bottom to top – and that was about all that let Ruby make any headway.

Showing over the top of the wall were the remains of very old buildings, mostly fallen down. The broken tops of walls were all rounded off. At the bottom of the wall and scattered down the slope were building stones that had fallen. There was the remains of an old two-story watchtower, just part of two corner walls showing, so far as I could see, and the *vigas*, the joists of the second floor and the roof rafters, were still there, big pine logs sticking out four feet or so.

To the right of the ancient walls and the old tower was a building that looked like it might have been made last week. It had a low T-shaped door and two windows, and it was about fifty feet long – made of selected, laid-up masonry that was brighter red than I'd seen in any other ruin. It had to be Red Ruin. The whole thing, the Red Ruin, about a hundred feet of ancient, broken-down walls, and the remains of the tower were on a flat floor in a deep cave about a hundred and fifty feet from floor to roof, and I'd say a hundred yards long. There was no back way out of it that I could see. Ruby had trapped himself.

I wondered what the hell he was doing, spread-eagled on that old retaining wall and making his way inch by inch up the crack, and liable to fall and break his neck any second. If he was heading for where he hid my money – and there couldn't be any other reason why he'd be there – he sure couldn't have climbed up that crack the night he rode in, in the near dark and freezing, with his fingers stiff as baling hooks. He'd have been crazy, with so many other hiding places around.

Then I saw why. I could see the old ledge or path that slanted across the talus slope and went up to the foot of the wall at one end. And there, the wall had fallen – a recent fall, probably undermined by the melting snow. And that had to be where the entrance used to be . . . a ramp, or Moqui handholds in the buttress cliff, or even a series of ladders. I could see where Ruby had tried to climb, and had slipped back bringing down more rocks and dirt. So the way he'd got up there with my money just wasn't there any more, and he was having trouble. He had his carbine hung on his belt by the saddle ring, and it kept getting in his way. He was knocking more building stones out of the old wall, but he was making progress.

This was my chance to get across to his side and lay for him right at the bottom of the wall when he climbed down again. He'd need both hands to keep from breaking his neck, and I'd have him cold. And right now, he was too busy hanging on to be looking over his shoulder. I got up from behind the log and ran across the sand and into the trees on his side. By the time I made my way through the cottonwoods and found a good place down behind some small rocks at the bottom of the slope, he was nearly at the top of the big wall. He didn't know I was there. In fact, far as he knew, I was a skeleton with a hole in the skull down by Junction Rock.

When he finally made it, he sat there resting with his legs dangling over the wall, and wiped the sweat off his face. Pretty soon he took the carbine off his belt and laid it beside him. I was close enough under the big wall, so I couldn't see much of the ancient ruins, except about a three-foot high wall behind Ruby and close to the edge – a kind of a parapet – and the old tower, which was right on the edge. All I could see of Red Ruin, which set farther back, was the *vigas*, and the parapet around the flat roof.

I got comfortable and settled in to wait. When he got through resting and went to get the money, he'd move back out of my sight beyond the edge of the cave. But that didn't matter, because he had to come to me. I had some fun picturing his face when he crawled back down that crack in the wall with both hands hanging on for life, and the man he'd left for dead two months ago would raise up and tell him, "Take it easy, Ruby. I wouldn't want you to slip and bring down the whole wall and bury my money." I wondered if he would fall off, just out of shock.

Then a dog barked, out on the sand. I turned and looked, and Mary's two dogs were nosing along Ruby's tracks, where he'd gone around a shoulder of the cliff. I heard Ruby swear, up above me. Then I saw Mary, ducking past an opening in the trees on the other side. She was carrying that old wreck of a carbine.

I started to yell at her, and just then Ruby fired, and the first dog flopped over and laid there kicking. It was a good shot, about a hundred yards and the dog moving.

I swung my carbine up and shot at Ruby, but way wide of the mark. I was too late, anyway, because he had thrown himself over the little wall at the edge of the cave, and all I saw was his feet disappearing. My shot knocked a couple of pieces of rock off the little wall, and they came bouncing down the high retaining wall.

Then I heard him run a few steps back from the wall, and out of my sight.

I thought, I hope she's got sense enough to keep out of sight. And what the hell do I do, now? He can fort up in there till dark, and I can't climb up to him. He'd nail me sure. Well, one thing he couldn't get down out of there, either, without my knowing it. He couldn't jump that forty feet down the face of the retaining wall without killing himself, and he couldn't climb down without me hearing him.

I stood up and waved my carbine for Mary

217

to go back. It was foolish to stand up that way, but I was afraid he'd shoot her ... and he damn near got me. His slug buzzed off my rock, stinging my left leg with chips, and I dropped flat on my face behind it. I couldn't see where he shot from. He had been out of sight, back from the edge of the cave. He didn't shoot again, and I figured he couldn't get a good enough angle to shoot down behind my rock.

I turned my head and saw Mary across there, looking around the trunk of a big cottonwood. I yelled for her to go away. Ruby shot at me again, then, and came damn close. Then I saw the smoke at the window of the second story of the old watch tower. He had climbed up there so he'd be high enough to see over the edge. I reached out, got four rocks the size of my head, and piled them up with a hole between for my carbine ... and had a pretty good shelter. I could still see the window in what was left of the near wall of the tower. I kept my sights on it. I had to get him before he got me or Mary or both. Had to keep him up there in the old tower, too, so he couldn't run the hundred feet and get into the Red Ruin, where the walls were thick and solid.

I kept watching the old window opening, staring so hard my eyes were watering. I yelled, "Better quit while you're ahead, Ruby! That means while you're still alive!"

He shot at me again. His shot burned a streak across my right boot, and I didn't even see him. He hollered, "Well I be God damn! Link Conway. I thought you were one of those Navvies! Remind me not to shoot you in the head again! I'll have to gut shoot you, this time."

The smoke gave him away again. He'd got onto what was left of the roof of the tower, which gave him a still better angle.

I got out of there. I ran, and made a dive under an over-hanging rock, where the talus slope butted against a piece of the cliff, at the left end of the big retaining wall. By squirming around, I could see the window in the second story of the tower and the roof, too, and I had room to shoot without showing more than my right eye and a piece of my right arm. I watched the roof, I guess there was just enough of it left for him to stretch out on it, and maybe the same area of floor still held up by the *vigas*, on the second story.

I yelled at him then, told him he was trapped and to throw his guns down, the carbine and his six-gun, and I wouldn't kill him. I said, "The derringer, too, this time!"

He had the nerve to laugh at me. He hollered, "I can stay forted up all day, up here. And you're stuck. I know just where you are, and if you so much as wiggle your ass, I've got you!"

Then, a lot closer than she had been, right square across from Red Ruin, Mary cut loose with that old Remington. She hit right on the corner where the walls joined, six or seven feet below where Ruby was, up on the roof behind the parapet. Two or three building stones jarred loose and fell out, and left a little cloud of powdered mortar dust hanging in the air. I squinted along my sights, ranging along the parapet, and didn't see Ruby. But he fired again, down at the window opening at the second floor this time, and I heard Mary scream.

I r'ared up, swearing at him, and he put one through my hat brim. I dropped back and skinned my face on a rock. He really had me pinned, like a frog on a gig. I'd have torn him apart with my bare hands if I could have reached him, but I wouldn't be able to use my hands if I was dead, and I didn't dare move.

I yelled, "Mary! Answer me!"

I nearly collapsed from relief when she answered, even though I couldn't understand what she said. At least, she was alive. Ruby took another shot at her, from the window again, and I raised up and shot through it, twice. He laughed at me.

I shot again, and knocked a couple of stones from the edge of the window opening, and I thought I saw the whole tower shiver a little. I couldn't be sure, through the smoke. Then I remembered how Mary's shot had knocked a chunk out of the corner, and how the building stones fell out of the retaining wall when Ruby was climbing it, and I knew there was something I could do if I had to.

I yelled, "Ruby! Last chance for you! Throw down your guns and come out."

I took a shot at the corner, where Mary had hit, and more stones fell out. Ruby yelled something, up on the roof. I thought he sounded scared.

Then he threw the six-gun down, clear out over the retaining wall so I'd be sure and see it. He hollered, "All right, Link! Don't shoot!"

I waited a few seconds, then felt around for a rock the size of my head, and rolled it out from behind my fort, down through some low bushes. It hadn't moved two feet when he pumped three shots as fast as he could work his carbine. Gravel and stones kicked up all around my rolling stone. He wasn't going to give up.

I yelled at him then that he had one more chance, to just throw down the carbine and the derringer.

He hollered, "Go to hell, you stupid bastard! I'm gonna cut you in two with 'em."

I yelled, "Okay, Ruby! That's it! You're long overdue!" and I filled the magazine of the carbine.

I aimed real careful at the edge of the window opening where I hit before, and fired. Flat rocks flew out, and there was a gouge in the side of the window opened two feet square, like something had taken a big bite out of it. Ruby hollered, but I didn't pay any attention. I hit the corner with the next one, on the same level at the window, and right where Mary had hit. Chips flew, and a heavy, square stone dropped. Some smaller ones spilled loose after it. Ruby yelled louder, and I guess he moved up there, maybe trying to scramble down. I figured where he might be, and shot halfway between the window and the corner, knocking a hole about a foot in diameter right through the wall. That ruin had been there maybe ten centuries, and it was now held together mostly by gravity. The whole thing shook, and the upper part swayed out just a hair, and settled back.

I began to switch, gouging chunks out of the corner, and then at the window opening, which was twice as wide now.

Ruby waved his hand above the parapet and yelled, and I shot a big hunk out of the parapet right where his hand had been. That was a waste, though, and I went back to undermining the whole upper story – the big gouge at the corner, then the bigger one at the window opening.

The whole top of the tower tipped outward a few inches and settled back. Then the whole front of it bellied out, pitched forward, and broke up into ten thousand separate building stones, one big mass without any shape. It crashed down onto the slope of the retaining wall, and just exploded. The retaining wall went, too, the whole length, curling over and breaking like a wave on a beach, and the whole shebang smashed onto the slope below and poured down it like a flash flood down a draw.

If Ruby hollered, I couldn't have heard him in that awful roar. And if he hadn't smoked me out of where I'd been and chased me past the end of the wall, I'd've been buried as deep as him.

Before it all stopped moving, while dirt and smaller rocks were still rolling and bouncing down where the wall had been, I dropped my carbine and ran down across the whole sliding pile. Small rocks bounced off my back and legs, and my feet kept slipping and sliding, and me half blind in the dust from the old dry mud mortar.

I ran through the fringe of cottonwoods and out onto the sand, calling her name. She walked out from the other side and met me. Tears were running down her face and I thought, well, things have changed, I guess.

I grabbed her arms and said, "Are you hurt? Are you shot, Mary?"

She rubbed her eyes and said, "He almost hit me. I was looking around a rock, and he knocked stone dust in my eyes."

Then, in spite of everything, and seeing her all right now, I couldn't pull her close the way I wanted. She was safe, and I was alive, but I'd been burned before, and I couldn't figure her out at all, and I didn't want her to spit in my face again.

I said, "Well, I'm glad you didn't get hurt."

I turned to look at where the wall had been, to look for a way to climb it. I couldn't see anything much. My eyes were blurry and I was all choked up, and not from the dust I'd swallowed.

And then she was around in front of me, looking up into my face, and she said, "Link! Oh, Link!" and shut her eyes and reached her arms out to me.

I guess I nearly squashed her, because after awhile she pulled her mouth away from mine and said, "I can't breathe." I loosened my arms, but she said, "Don't let go! Just give me time to take a breath!"

We were both laughing, only she was crying at the same time.

CHAPTER 13

After a while she backed off a little, and looked into my eyes for a long time. I said, "What is it, Mary?"

"Nothing," she said, and reached out and took my hand.

My knees were shaky. Not because of killing Ruby. I hadn't ever killed a man, hadn't ever even shot at one in my life, till that morning when Johnny Moore and Joe Ochoa pushed those syndicate cows onto my section. I took a shot at Johnny that morning, and I thought at the time, I guess, that I wasn't shooting to miss. But I don't miss very often, and I've thought since, that something kept me from laying my front sight on his head. Anyway, I wouldn't have killed Ruby, maybe, even if I couldn't have beat it out of him where he hid the money. But my skin crawled when I remembered how he had shot at Mary and I heard her scream. I'd have had the shakes over how close he came to killing me, but that didn't even enter my mind, now ... just the thought of her being shot. And I didn't regret Ruby Blair for one second, because if I hadn't knocked that tower down with him in it, he might not have missed next time he shot at her.

"Why the hell didn't you go back when I told you?" I said.

"He was shooting at you!" she said. "Twice, when he shot and you didn't move, I thought he hit you. You think I could just turn my back and go home, and not know if you were dead?"

I grabbed her again, and she laid her face against mine for a few seconds, then she said, "And after all this, you lost your money.

226

You'll never be able to dig him out of that heap of rocks."

"If he had it on him, I'd dig him out," I said. "But he never had time to get it. He was climbing up that wall, not coming down, when I first saw him. It's up there somewhere in those ruins."

"The tower's gone," she said. "Maybe that's where it was. That's where he went first, wasn't it?"

"That don't mean anything," I said. "He had to get higher so he could get a shot at me." But I began to worry. Maybe he figured when he hid the money, that the first place anyone would look, if it ever came to that, would be in Red Ruin, that had tight walls and a good solid roof, and he was cagey and hid it in the tower instead.

"Come on," I said. "Let's go look."

She said, "No, I'll wait for you."

Then I remembered she was scared to go in any ruin, with maybe mummies buried under the floor and old Anasazi ghosts flitting around.

She walked with me over to the edge of the trees, but she wouldn't go any farther. When I began to climb the talus slope beside that big jumble of rock with Ruby Blair somewhere under it, I looked back. She was scooping a hole in the sand for the dead dog, and chasing

227

the other one away from it.

I picked up my carbine, wiped it off, and leaned it against a rock.

Just about the whole area where the retaining wall had been was swept clean, and there didn't seem to be any way to get up to the cave. I finally made it by finding a slanting fault in the cliff that went up past the cave, about forty feet away, and then a ledge that went across the cliff face. A couple of times I thought I was a goner when my foot slipped. My fingers were bleeding when I got up there, but I made it.

It was creepy in that big cave, even in broad daylight. Rain and snow never got in there, and there were *metates* worn almost through by years of grinding corn, the flat *mano* stones near them, painted pots, and a million potsherds. Except for the dust, it looked like people had left there five minutes ago. There were a couple of yucca fiber sandals, and arrow points, and an arrow straightener, and a bundle of cane arrow shafts tied up with yucca fiber string. What really gave me the chills, though, was where the falling wall had carried a part of the edge of the cave floor with it, where packed dirt was four feet deep from thousands of years of dust blowing in, before anybody ever lived there. It had opened up two graves, right under

228

where people had sat and wove baskets and chipped arrow points. They were just holes scooped in the ground and covered with slabs of broken sandstone, like flagstones. One had a small skeleton wrapped in rotted old tatters of a woven blanket. It had clam shell bracelets still on the wrist bones, and some of the hair still stuck on the skull. Beside it was a skeleton I thought first must be a rabbit, but the little skull was human. In the other grave a skeleton was lying on its side with the arms crossed and the knees bent up to the ribs, and the skull covered with a big pottery bowl with a hole in it. I wouldn't have touched them for anything.

If Ruby had ever left any tracks in the dust on the floor of the cave, they had been scattered or covered up by wind, and I didn't waste any time looking around there. I walked around old walls, past a couple of small rooms with the roofs gone, and a fire pit with charcoal, burned deer bones, and pieces of mescal leaves in it.

I went into the Red Ruin, ducking low to go through the T-shaped doorway, and inside there it was even creepier. I began to feel like I'd go into the next room and come face to face with some thousand-year-old hunter in a rabbit-fur blanket, carrying a spear and spear thrower. There were little corncobs about three inches long lying around, and a *metate* that still had traces of corn meal in the lava grinding surface. And there was a wad of cotton and a spindle, and in the corner, what was left of a waist loom just like Lieutenant Haverhill had taken out of Ram House Ruin two years ago. There were pack rat tracks and droppings all over the place. Anyway, in the dust on the floor I found boot tracks. Ruby had been there!

But not today, because I'd caught up with him before he climbed the wall.

In a corner I found the remains of a fire ... dead cottonwood limbs charred on the ends and still bright where he'd broke them up. What clinched it, though, was the empty Bull Durham sack. That hadn't been there any thousand years!

I hunted through that room for an hour, looking for places where he might have dug a hole, reaching up and feeling along the roof *vigas* – I even dug into the firepit – and I didn't find one sign of my money belt. I gave up and went into the next room, and Ruby's tracks were there, too. It was dark, with only the light from one little window opening. There was the same kind of stuff in there – *metates* and *manos,* a lot of flint and obsidian chips where they had chipped arrowheads with a piece of deer antler. In one corner was a big *olla*, at least three feet in diameter, and beside it a bunch of potsherds where another big pot had been broken. I didn't look in the pot because Ruby's tracks didn't go near that corner.

Just when I was about to give up looking, and see if there was another room, I noticed something. The dirt floor had been swept all around that big pot. I could barely make it out, scratchy looking marks made by a branch or a bundle of yucca fiber or something, and the dust almost hiding the marks where he had brushed away his tracks.

I dumped the big *olla* over and it smashed. About two bushels of corncobs, seed shells, and rat droppings spilled out . . . and there was my green, oiled-silk money belt.

Rats had chewed on it, and when I took the bills out, some of them were chewed on one corner. But it was all there, sixty-three hundred-dollar bills.

It didn't take me long to get down out of there. It's a wonder I didn't break a leg. I ran across the floor of the cave to the edge where the wall had fallen, and slid on my rump down the exposed earth. It was full of pieces of building stones, and I got some bruises. When I got to that heap of rubble over Ruby Blair, I almost ran across it. Then I remembered my carbine, and had to go back and get it where I'd leaned it on the rock.

I ran across to Mary, where she was waiting by the heap of sand where she'd buried the dog, grabbed her, swung her off her feet, whirled her around, and set her down. I kissed her hard, and said, "Ram House Trading Post, here I come!"

She didn't get excited at all. I guess because while she wasn't rich, she had what money she needed. She wouldn't know what it meant to a forty-a-month cowboy to have all that money. She said, "I'm glad, Link. Was it all worth while? Getting yourself shot, and killing a man?"

I said, "Killing him doesn't bother me, Mary. I'd have let him go if he'd let me. He tried his best to kill me, at least twice. Even then, I wouldn't have killed him if he hadn't shot at you! And believe me, the rest of it was worth it! If I'd known I had to get shot to meet you and stay with you all that time, and what it would get to mean to me, I'd have done it."

"Would you, Link?" she said. "Well, let's go back. There's still time for you to get to Chinle this afternoon."

"You so anxious to get rid of me?" I said, just joking, and I folded the money belt and put it inside my shirt and took her arm. She didn't pull away, but she didn't squeeze my hand against her, or anything like that. I thought she was giving me the chance to leave right now if I wanted, and show me she wasn't trying to hold onto me. Because she must know, now – as I did – that I loved her.

Then I saw that she meant it. She really wanted me to go. Or if she didn't she gave an awful good imitation. She didn't smile or talk when we walked back to the hogan. I didn't know what to make of her at all, or whether she didn't like me, or was afraid to show she did for fear she'd get hurt again. She'd been hurt by about everyone she ever met except Old Man Beasley . . . even by her own people. I'd been a lot of bother and trouble to her, and I couldn't help that, when I was shot.

I fed and watered the three horses, then took the saddle, bridle, and saddlebags into the hogan.

She made fried bread and we opened the last can of corned beef, and now she wouldn't even look at me. After we ate, I took her in my arms and said, "Mary, what did I do?" I tried to kiss her, but it was like kissing a carved, wooden statue and I quit.

All she would say, when I kept pushing at her, was that now I had my money and I could buy the trading post, and I'd be happy.

She stood around doing nothing, and I knew she was waiting for me to go . . . but

I couldn't leave it like that.

I said, "You're going to drive in tomorrow, aren't you?"

She nodded, and I said, "Well, I'm going to stay tonight. I'll ride in with you."

"I can't make you go," she said, "But you aren't going to stay in here."

I grinned at her then. "All right," I said. "We can be real cozy in the wagon again."

She didn't smile or say anything. I spent most of the afternoon chopping wood, greasing the wagon, and checking over her harness. It got dark early, about five o'clock, and she had a good dinner ready – the last of the fresh mutton and a real good dried-peach pie she baked in a dutch oven.

I didn't try to kiss her goodnight when I took the sheepskins out to the wagon. I was sure she'd come out to me again. I laid there thinking about owning the Ram House Trading Post and living there with her, and having a bunch of kids that I never thought I'd ever want before. It got later and later and I was dog tired, and I finally went to sleep. She never did come.

It was a broad daylight when I woke up, and smoke was pouring out of the smoke hole of the hogan. I pulled on my boots, folded the blankets, and went over. My saddle and gear were piled outside, and the door was fastened. I knocked, but she didn't answer.

I said, "Hey, I'm up! Why didn't you call me?"

She said, "You go ahead. I'm not going."

"What's the matter with you!" I said. "We were going together."

"I changed my mind," was all she'd say, and I stood there not knowing what to do.

Finally I said, "How about a cup of coffee, then?"

"You can get it at Chinle, when you go out," she said, and I couldn't get another thing out of her. I put the blankets and sheepskins down and sat on them, and waited half an hour. Finally, I saddled up and rode out. I kept looking back till I rounded a bend and couldn't see the hogan any more.

I guess, in spite of her, I should have been excited about getting my money back, but I wasn't, somehow. I was discouraged and low, and I sure didn't want to leave that canyon and what I had found down there beside Ruby Blair and my sixty-three hundred dollars. And now I wasn't even sure I wanted the Ram House Trading Post. I thought I could do like Old Man Beasley when he first came, and run the post even if I didn't know Navajo. Franklin Yazzie and I liked each other, and I thought he'd be glad to stay on with me, if Old Man Beasley did sell to me and go to California. But thinking about Mary left an ache in my middle that I'd be a long time getting over, and if I was there in the post the way I'd been picturing myself, I'd run into Mary time and again, and I wouldn't be able to stand that. I thought I knew what was bothering her ... she just didn't trust me, or any white man, or anyone else, or believe I meant what I said. Well, she had her reasons for that, and I could understand it ... but not to trust me?

But then, maybe she was telling the truth when she had said the next morning that it didn't mean a thing to her except a little fun in the blankets. Even that she didn't care if she had a kid because it would be all hers, not mine in any way, or me having any claim on it. I guess I'm a fool where women are concerned. Look how easy Callie had fooled me. But to my mind, it looked like Mary should trust me, and I still thought she loved me or she wouldn't ever have climbed into bed with me, no matter what she said about the different way Navajos looked at it. Well, I thought, what makes sense to a man is something else to a woman, and if she's half Indian, you'll never know what's going on in her head. That didn't make it any easier to ride away from her, though. It was like I'd torn off half of me and left it there in that hogan, and I didn't have anything to fill the big hole it left.

Then it struck me I hadn't ever asked her to marry me. Maybe that was the hitch. I almost turned back. But then, I knew she had to know I meant that, because she knew I loved her. Or if she didn't know it by now, she never would.

I decided to get Old Man Beasley's horse at the hogan where Ruby killed Hosteen Lichee, and take it back to the old man. Maybe I'd stay with him a day or two till I figured out what I was going to do.

Riding up the long, easy grade that topped out near Chinle, I passed three Navajo wagons coming down into the canyon for the spring and summer and I had to wait while two Navajo women and six dogs pushed a lot of sheep and goats along on their way down. I didn't want to stop at Sam Day's trading post in Chinle and answer a lot of questions. I didn't want to talk to anybody, so I rode wide around Chinle and cut back to the road. It took me a while to find the hogan, and when I did, it was burned down. The corral was still there, but nobody had been there for a long time. I'd forgot the Navajos are scared to death of spirits, and sometimes burn down a hogan where somebody died, or chop a hole in the west side and take the body out.

So I rode back to Sam Day's place. He was surprised to see me. Nobody had seen me since that day Ruby rode into the canyon trying to get away from that Navajo posse. Everybody figured I'd just rode back out that night, and gone away.

I didn't tell him anything. I had come into Chinle from the direction of the road, so he didn't know I'd just come out of Canyon de Chelly . . . and I just didn't want to make a lot of explanations.

I said, "What happened to Beasley's horse I left at Hosteen Lichee's hogan that day?"

"Oh, I knew it was his," he said. "I took it back to him."

"How is he?"

"Haven't seen him since then. Snow's been too deep. He wasn't feeling so good after that whack on the head, but Old Beasley's too ornery to let a little winter weather get him. I guess you heard, Blair got clean away. The Navvies found his tracks where he came up that trail opposite the White House. You find any trace of him?"

"I think I know where to find him," I said, and let it go at that. "Well, so long, see you some time. If you see Hosteen Lichee's kid, tell him I'll leave the horse with Beasley."

About three in the afternoon, I turned into the road that ran to the Ram House Trading Post from the Ganado-Round Rock road. When I came over the rise and looked down, there was a Navajo wagon just leaving, and nobody else in sight. But one thing made me feel good – the first thing that day for sure! There was old Sox in the corral, standing nose to tail with Beasley's team horses.

There were three Indian horses at the hitchrack. I unsaddled, slung my saddle and saddlebags over the rack, and led the horse down to the corral. I looked Sox over, and he looked good, even with all that winter fur on him. I slapped him on the chest and scratched under his chin, but he didn't act like I'd even been away. I went back and slung my saddlebags over my arm and picked up my saddle and went in.

There were two old long-hairs and a big fat squaw at the counter. They looked at me, squinting in the lamp light, and the squaw sort of hissed, *"Chindee!"* and the three of them ran out of there like the devil was on their trail. They must have heard I was dead.

But I didn't pay any attention, because there was Callie behind the counter.

CHAPTER 14

I don't know who was the most surprised, but I guess she was, even though she was the last person in the world I expected to see there, after what she'd done to me and Old Man Beasley. Her face went white, and she backed up against the shelves and stared at me. I guess she thought I was a ghost. She gulped and started to say something, but she couldn't get it out.

I dropped the saddle and walked past her, and she shrunk back away from me, her eyes about popping out of her head. I went through the kitchen and into Old Man Beasley's room. He had an overcoat on over his long red underwear, and was sitting at his table by the window, going through a ledger. He looked ten years older, his cheeks sunk in under his scraggly beard, and his knobby old hands trembling. He didn't look up. He said, "On top of everything else, you're a thief, and I can prove it."

I said, "What the hell are you talking about?"

He jerked his head up and looked at me. His eyes were red rimmed and sunk in his

240

head. "God sakes!" he said. "It's you! I thought you was dead! The Navvies said you went down Canyon de Chelly after that son of a bitch, an' he come out an' you didn't!" He dropped the ledger and got up and took my hand in both of his. "Mighty glad to see you, boy! When you come in, I thought you was her. Then I didn't scarcely reco'nize you with that beard."

"What's she doing here?" I said.

"He left her high and dry," Beasley said. "Not a cent to her name, no place to go. She ain't got a friend in the world."

"And she was such a nice, pretty little girl ... about fifteen years ago, is that it?" I said.

"Guess that's part of it."

Callie came in then, and stood inside the door. "Link," she said, "I ... we waited and waited. I thought you were dead ... Oh, Link, I'm so glad, so glad!"

She held out her hands to me, and I said, "Cut it out, Callie!"

She bit her lower lip, and stepped back, and tears came into her eyes.

Beasley said, "Well, I couldn't kick her out in the dead of winter, could I? Couldn't let her starve, could I?"

"Who couldn't let who starve?" Callie said. "Who'd've run the place for you, with you laid up with the rheumatism?"

241

She turned and smiled at me, kind of trembly, like a kicked dog crawling back for more. "I'm really glad, Link! I thought Ruby killed you."

"Well, don't low-rate him for not doing it, he sure tried. And I don't just mean right here, with your help."

She sniffled and wiped her nose, and looked so beat down, I almost began to feel sorry for her, and I thought, Hold on there, Link, boy! Watch it! She's poison!

Old Man Beasley went on with the argument like there hadn't been any interruption ... like it had been going on for days, "Wasn't the rheumatism laid me up! That husband of yours done it with a gun. Thievin' an' robbin' an' tryin' to murder people. An' you with him all the way!"

"He made me, and you know it!" Callie said. She didn't look so good, either. Her hair was straggly and dirty, and no paint or powder on her face, and lines running past the corners of her mouth. Her shirtwaist wasn't ironed and wasn't too clean, either.

"I could've walked out on you!" she went on. "Then who'd've taken care of your stinking Navvies all winter, an' cooked for you and kept the place running?"

"Franklin Yazzie, that's who!" he said. "Only you run him off. Fightin' with him an' orderin' him around an' tellin' him he's no good. So's you wouldn't have anybody out there with you in the bull pen with me laid up, and nobody could see you stealin' from the till."

"You quit saying that! It's a dirty lie!"

"That so? Guess I can check the books, can't I? I can see how much stock got sold and how much you put down in the debits an' credits."

"They steal! Just me out there, and maybe twenty stinking Navvies sometimes. How do you expect me to watch everybody at once?"

"Aw, shut up! Go get supper!"

She sniffed and blew her nose, and turned to me. "We heard Ruby got away from you, and you were dead. I'm glad you're not, Link. I'm glad you got back. Where have you been? You find any trace of him?"

"No." I didn't want to talk to her.

"I'll lock up and get supper." She stood there looking at me a minute, then she said, "The Navvies said he was hanging around Gallup in December and January, then he went away. I don't know why he'd do that, with all that money. If I know him, he's back east somewhere, or maybe New Orleans."

She went out, then.

Beasley said, "I don't know what I'm gonna do, Link. I can't run the place no more. I

243

would've sold out to you ... five thousand, like you said. I was just hagglin', that's all. And now that's all done." And he went to swearing at Ruby and Callie.

I didn't want to tell him anything, with her within hearing distance.

He said, "Well, maybe you'd stay around and help out. You ain't got anything, either. I could talk to the Navvies and you could do the work. I'd cut you in for a share."

"I don't know. Maybe I'll think about it."

He came out to the kitchen for supper, and none of us talked. He went to his bedroom, after, and shut the door.

I carried in some wood and filled the water tank. Callie sat at the table, and when I got my saddle and started to go put it in my room, she said "Sit down a minute, Link."

I put my gear away, got a sack of Bull Durham, and rolled my first smoke in nearly three months. She looked across the table at me, and said, "Link, it wasn't my fault. You don't know how he was. I was always scared of him, but I couldn't get away from him. He said he'd kill me. He wouldn't let me tell anybody we were married, in Prescott. He told me to play up to the ranchers and the mine owners, and we'd find a sucker and make a stake. And when you got that money ... I didn't want to, Link. You've got to believe me! He made me do it all. And I liked you, Link! You know that's true, or I wouldn't ever have . . . well, I wouldn't have slept with you that night. And you liked me, Link. I know you did."

I just wanted to get away from her. "You're wasting your time, Callie. I haven't got the money any more. Your husband robbed me. So what's the use to talk?" And I got up and went into the bedroom.

I could hear her crying . . . not bawling for my benefit, just sniffling to herself. I looked out, and she had her head down on the table, and her shoulders were shaking. I almost went out to tell her to forget it, that it was all over and done. I shut the door, then got my razor and shaved my beard off, and went to bed. My face felt funny without it.

It was pretty gloomy around there for the next few days, with nobody saying a decent word to anybody else, Beasley and her bickering, and no customers coming in. Beasley said the Navajos probably thought I was a ghost, and if he didn't change their minds, they'd never come near the place again. He said when he felt a little better he'd get hold of Franklin Yazzie and tell him I'd just been away hunting for Ruby Blair. Yazzie would spread the word, and they'd start coming back.

Callie told me how to stock the shelves, and I hauled wood and water, took care of the horses, and took Sox out for a couple of long rides. I don't know why I didn't just pull stakes for somewhere, but I hadn't made up my mind about where I wanted to go. I even thought I might buy the place after all. If I'd never met Mary Wilson, it would have been exactly what I wanted to do, and I knew I could buy it for five thousand now, and have some working capital left over. But then I knew it was spoiled for me, for good. I guess I hung around in hopes I'd see her once more. That maybe she'd had a chance to think it over, and would miss me as bad as I missed her. Maybe, too, I'd find out that even if she wouldn't marry me, it would be enough just to see her once in a while. Maybe after while, we could be friends, anyway.

But she didn't come. And I figured she had done her trading at Chinle with Sam Day, and wouldn't come to the Ram House Post as long as she knew I was there.

Then Franklin Yazzie drove in with his wagon and a new bride. She was a pretty, little, brown girl so bashful she wouldn't even look at me, but put her hand over her mouth, the way they do when they're embarrassed. Yazzie asked me a lot of questions about where I'd been all winter, and didn't look like he quite believed me when I told him I'd been hunting for Ruby Blair. The Navajos had ways of knowing things none of them had even seen happen, and nobody knows how they do it. He said that somebody'd heard a lot of shooting down in the canyon a few days ago. "They say . . ." he would say. Or, "It is said . . ." the way they do. Nobody ever says, "Ki-Neez told me," or "Natai was talking the other day." The same way they don't call a man by his name, or point at him.

Callie didn't say a word to Yazzie, but Old Man Beasley said right in front of her, "Frankie, she won't be around long. You come back to work for me. I'll give you one of the hogans to live in."

Franklin grinned at him and said, "Sure. We bring our stuff tomorrow and put it in hogan." He and his bride had coffee and a can of tomatoes and went out.

I went out, too. It was a pretty warm night for that time of year, and the stars were out. Even with no moon, you could see things, the stars were so bright. I went down and talked to Sox for a while, until I figured Callie and Beasley would have gone to bed. Then I went in and locked the door. Callie had left a lamp lit for me.

I pulled my boots off and went to her door in my sock feet. There wasn't any light

247

showing under her door, and I couldn't hear her stirring around or the bed creaking, so I went to Beasley's room. I could hear him muttering and mumbling in there, and I thought he was awake, but when I eased the door open, he was having a dream, and tossing around. I went in, put the lantern on the table and sat in a chair and waited. Pretty soon the light bothered him, and he sat up and looked at me with his hair all on end.

"I want to talk to you."

"Git me my overcoat," he said. "Any coffee left?"

I tiptoed out to the kitchen and poured two cups of coffee from the pot on the back of the stove, and when I went back he had his overcoat and some wool socks on, and was sitting at the table.

I sat on the bed. "Now don't talk loud. I got my money back."

He kind of jumped, and said, "What?" real loud.

"Shut up! She's asleep."

"My God! Where'd you catch up with him?"

"In Red Ruin, down in Canyon de Chelly," I told him. "He's still there, under fifty tons of rocks. That's what I want to talk about."

"Wished I'd've been there to see it," he said, and then he sat there and forgot his coffee. He didn't say a word while I told him the whole thing. Only I didn't tell him how I felt about Mary. Then I said, "That is what's bothering me. I guess I've got to report this death and how it happened. What do you think?"

He sat pulling at his lower lip a while. He said, then, "Nobody knows about it but Mary, and you know her, she'll never tell anybody. Wouldn't even tell me. Nor no other Navvie will, either. It's white man's business, and they don't care who got killed. No, nobody'll ever say a word. Far as you're concerned, he robbed you and tried to kill you. He already done one murder, and God knows how many others back along his trail. The law'd be nothin' but happy to forget all about Ruby Blair. If I was you, I'd forget it, too. You report it, and they got to investigate and maybe hold a trial, and God knows how long you'll be tangled up in it. He ain't the first that came onto the reservation and never went off it. And who's to ask about him? Nobody but Callie, even if she knew. And I don't think she would, after what he done to her." He drank his cold coffee then, and said, "Well, like I said, Link, I ain't gonna haggle. Five thousand it is. And now the weather's gettin' better, I'll stay around a while and get you started, and you got Franklin Yazzie to do the talkin'. An' his wife to do the cleanin' an' cookin', if you can learn her to." He laughed again, and said, "Californy, here I come! Santa Barb'ry or bust!"

"I don't know. I think maybe I changed my mind."

That hauled him up short. He sputtered some and puffed out his lips. Then he said, "I got the picture, I guess . . . but you're makin' a mountain out of a mole hill. Link, Mary's like my own daughter. Ain't much I wouldn't do for her, like takin' a shotgun to you. But I guess I can't blame you, human nature bein' what it is . . . yours an' hers, too. So it'd be agin' nature for you to live there with her all that time and not try to get her into your blankets. An' likely she didn't try very hard to hold you off, bein' lonesome like she is, and young and lively. So now you figure if you buy the place, she'll be comin' around all the time, and maybe think she's got a claim on you, and you'll be ashamed to face her and won't know how to handle it. Well, you got nothing to worry about. You don't know the Navvies, Link. It don't mean a thing to them. Why, I remember . . . well, let's say I wasn't much older'n you when I come here, an' there was all these pretty little girls around. Well, no matter. I wouldn't doubt, seein' what happened, she'd come around nights once in

250

a while, after you lock up. Might even move right in with you. So you see, that's a little something throwed in that you never expected to buy with the place."

I let him run down. I'd been getting madder the longer he talked. I said, "Beasley, you're a dirty old man. It's her that won't have me! And that's the whole reason I wouldn't buy your place for five dollars, let alone five thousand."

I got up and shoved the door open. It banged into something and I shoved it harder. It was Callie shivering in her nightgown, staring at me with her mouth open. I almost knocked her down when I rammed my way past and out through the bull pen. I went outside, put a halter on Sox and tied the rope for a rein, and took a long ride. I did a lot of thinking, but it just went in circles and I still didn't know what I wanted to do.

When I came back, locked up, and went to my room, Callie had her door open a crack. She whispered, "Link! Just a minute, Link!" but I went on into my room and shut the door.

CHAPTER 15

I got up early and built up the fire. There were dirty dishes from supper the night before, and I did them up and then got breakfast. Old Man Beasley came out and went to the two-holer back of the warehouse. He came in and warmed his skinny old butt in front of the stove before he sat down at the table, and piled six hotcakes on his plate with about a pint of corn syrup. He said, "Now about you buyin' the place, boy, why I wouldn't let Mary Wilson throw me off. How many posts you think are for sale on the reservation, anyway? You'll never get a chance like . . ." and he broke off and stopped chewing and talking at the same time, and stared behind me.

I looked around and Callie said, "Good morning!" bright and cheery as a bird. She had on a new skirt and a white, long-sleeved blouse with lace on the collar. She smelled like a combination of mothballs and lavender. Her hair was curled and done up on top of her head, and she had rouge and powder on, and her mouth was red. She smiled and sat down, and said, "My, this looks good! I didn't know you could cook, Link!"

252

For a woman that just found out last night that her husband was dead, and buried under tons of rock in the bottom of a canyon, she looked pretty chipper. She sure didn't look like a liar and a cheat and a thief.

Beasley said, "You watch out, Link! She's gettin' set to strike, and her kind don't rattle first!"

She looked like she wanted to kill him, then she smiled and patted his hairy old cheek, and said, "My, you're a sweet old man! Just full of jokes this morning, aren't you!" She turned to me. "I want to talk to you after breakfast, Link."

"What about? We've got nothing to talk about."

"Oh, yes, we do! I don't want to bring any pressure to bear, and I'm not trying to threaten you, but you killed my husband, Link ... and we can't just forget a killing like it didn't happen, can we? I'm afraid I have to report it. But I wouldn't do it without talking it over with you first."

"All right, Callie, start talking. What kind of blackmail are you figuring on?"

"Not in front of him," she said, and nodded her head at Beasley. "And don't you dare say blackmail! I'm giving you every consideration! That's why I'm giving you a chance to talk it over."

I laughed at her. Old Man Beasley said, "Jee-sus! I knew you had gall, but I never knew even *you'd* have the guts to ... God A'mighty!"

"You keep out of this, you filthy old bastard!" She was snarling like a cornered weasel.

I said, "I'll report it myself, then. I never killed Ruby. He was trying his best to kill me, and Mary, too, when that ruin collapsed. You heard it all, standing there in the hall when I told Beasley about it last night. If they ever dug him up, they wouldn't find any slugs in him. He robbed me and tried to kill me twice, and maybe more. Mary saw the whole thing!"

"Mary!" she said, like she was spitting. "Who'd believe her?"

"Who'd believe you!" Beasley said. "Listen, you ... you..." He couldn't think of anything bad enough. "You're what they call an accessory, don't you know that? Who sent Link up here? Who sneaked, and pried, and listened, and found out where he kept his money? Who tolled Ruby in here and showed him where it was? Who stood by when he slugged me and near killed me? You stupid painted fool, you'll do ten years in the penitentiary!"

"Link!" she said. "Don't let him talk like that! You know I couldn't help it! You know he made me do it. He'd have killed me if I didn't! Link! You wouldn't tell them I ... I was to blame for what Ruby did?"

I said, "Not unless you force me to. I got my money back, and Ruby's dead. But you lay any charges against me, Callie, you tell any more lies, and the whole thing will come out. You wouldn't have stopped at killing me any more than Ruby did."

Her face went white, and the rouge spots stood out like two red dollars.

"You hate me, don't you!" she said, real sad. "I can't even trust you!" She got up, ran to her room down the hall, and slammed the door.

Beasley said, "Jesus God! You know, I think she ain't right in the head."

She had me kind of sick to my stomach, too. She wasn't sorry, not for anything. And I guess she honestly couldn't see where she'd done anything wrong.

Beasley sat there shaking his head. I got up and said, "You want me to open the bull pen?"

"Might as well, but there won't be any customers till I get Franklin Yazzie started makin' the rounds to tell 'em you ain't a ghost."

"It don't matter. I'll be leaving today, I guess."

255

"You ain't gonna buy, then?" He looked like I'd hit him, too. "Even if I was to shave the price a little more?"

"I don't think so. Too much happened up here. I guess I just want to forget it all."

"You mean Mary Wilson?" he said.

"Yes," I said. "that's it, mostly."

I went out, unlocked the bull pen, and built up the fire. Beasley came out and began to check over the credit and charges on the paper bags. After I fed the horses, I came back and did a little work, stocking the shelves, filling small paper sacks with flour and sugar from the big sacks, and straightening things up. I knew I'd ought to pack my gear and ride out if I was going to get to Ganado before dark, but I couldn't quite bring myself to cut the last ties and shove it all behind me. We went in and had some lunch. Callie didn't come out of her room. Then Beasley said he thought he'd lay down for a while, and went to his room.

I went back into the bull pen and sat on a stack of rugs, just so somebody'd be there if any Navajos showed up. Pretty soon Callie came out.

She started to say something, but the door opened and Franklin Yazzie and his wife came in. He said, "Hey, Link. We gonna go back to my hogan and get our stuff. Tell old man we comin' back tonight, huh?"

Callie walked around, poking at things on the shelves and looking at them and putting them back, until Yazzie went out.

I didn't want to talk to her any more, and I got up and started to go outside. I heard Yazzie talking to somebody, and horses walking, and the rattle of the wagon.

Callie said, "Wait a minute, Link. Please!"

"I got nothing to say to you."

She came over and took my arm in both hands, and said, "You don't really hate me, do you Link? I told you and told you it was all Ruby's doing, and I couldn't help it. He made me help him, Link!"

"I heard you. Callie, I don't know how you had the nerve to stay here, after what you did. I don't want to talk to you." I started to move away, but she hung on to my arm.

"Why, I couldn't leave! Who would keep the place running? Beasley was laid up, and the Navajos have to have the place open so they can get what they need. You know that! You can't ever close up a trading post. You'd lose your license."

"Maybe that was it, and maybe not. You didn't have any place to go and no money, and Beasley let you stay."

"You just won't believe anything I say, will you," she said. "You won't give me a chance.

You used to like me, Link." She began to cry, then, and said, "You hate me! Well, I guess I can't blame you. But if you only knew . . ."

She was sniffling, so I gave her my bandanna. She wiped her eyes, and blew her nose. Then she hugged my arm, put her head on my shoulder, and said, "I never did love him, Link. I married him just to get away from my father . . . and I didn't want to do the things he made me do, but I was so afraid of him. And the reason he hated you, Link, he knew . . ." She stopped and blew her nose again.

"All right, Callie, I don't want to talk about it. I'm going to leave."

"Wait, Link! You don't know!"

"Know what?"

"I fell in love with you, and Ruby knew it, and that's why he hated you and tried to kill you. I always liked you, Link, and then when you came up here, I missed you something awful, and I came after you because I couldn't stand not to."

I pushed away from her then, but she grabbed my arm again.

"The only thing you came for was to set it up so he could rob me. You told us so, yourself, me and Beasley. And now I've got the money back, you're after me again."

I felt cold air coming in the door, and I

thought Franklin Yazzie hadn't closed it. I was going to go over and shut it, but Callie said, "Oh, no! Link! That isn't it at all! Link, buy the place. It's what you want. And I'll stay. I'll live with you ... you don't have to marry me! And I know how to run the place, and I'll teach you Navajo. And then if it doesn't work out, why I'll go away and never bother you again."

From the door to the kitchen, Old Man Beasley said, "God sakes, Link, you ain't gonna listen to her, are you? You'd as soon put a sidewinder in your pocket! Listen, boy, you can run the place easy, with Franklin Yazzie to help."

Callie said, "I bet it's that half-breed you spent the winter with. You went crazy for her, didn't you? Well, I don't mind that, Link. It won't make any difference to me. If she comes around here, I know how to run her off."

I shoved her away, then. I was sick of the two of them. "You're damn right I'm crazy about her! You ain't fit to touch her. If she'd have me, I'd marry her today!"

Well, Mary had been standing over by the door I don't know how long, and heard it all. I guess it was her I'd heard Yazzie talking to outside. She came over to us, but she didn't look at me.

She said, "Mr. Beasley, how long since you

259

looked at your pawn jewelry?"

"Huh? What's that? What you talking about, Mary?"

"She's been stealing it."

"Why, you half-breed whore!" Callie said. "You've got the nerve to spend the whole winter sleeping with Link, and then come in here and accuse me of . . .!"

"What the hell is this, Mary?" Beasley said.

"Hashke Nahba drove down into the canyon yesterday with his family," Mary said. "He told me she stole the best pieces of pawn. All the Navajos know it's gone, since she's been running the post alone."

"Well, now, by God!" Beasley said, and went stumping over to the pawn room, and turned the knob, but the door was locked. He held his hand out and said, "Callie, gimme the key. And don't say you ain't got it. I give it to you when I was laid up, and you took them two bracelets in pawn."

Callie snarled, "You lying, half-breed whore!" and went for Mary, getting hold of the chongo knot of her hair and jerking her head back and forth. I jumped in to pull her off and got an elbow in the mouth and a kick in the shin. Old Man Beasley was doddering around and cussing, and me circling around looking for a handhold. Mary put her left hand in Callie's face, shoved her against the shelves, and stepped back. They were both hunched over, breathing hard, getting set to go at it again. I stepped in between them and shoved them farther apart. Callie was swearing and calling Mary dirtier names than I'd ever heard any woman use before.

I got in between them, and Callie tried to dodge around me and get at Mary again. I grabbed her shoulders and pushed her against the wall and held her there, twisting and struggling. I couldn't watch them both, and lost track of Mary for a few seconds, and the next thing I knew, Old Man Beasley was yelling, "No! Adezhbah! None of that, now!" Mary slid under my arm and got between me and Callie. She had ducked into the kitchen, and had a butcher knife in her hand. She stuck the point against the base of Callie's throat, and said to me, over her shoulder, "Get back, Link, or I shove it in!"

I was tempted to grab her, but I didn't dare. First move I'd make she'd cut Callie's throat. I stepped back. I said, "Mary, if you . . ." but I didn't know any threat that would stop her.

Callie's eyes were about popping out of her head, and she was shoving back hard against the wall, trying to get away from that knife point. She whispered so I could barely hear her, "Mary! Please, Mary!"

261

Mary ripped out and downward with the knife, and it cut loose the top of Callie's shirtwaist and a couple of shoulder straps that were holding up some kind of underwear. Her right shoulder and part of her chest were bare.

Callie was about to faint, and I felt queazy myself, because we both sure thought she was gonna be stuck like a pig. She gulped and tried to talk, but just sort of squeaked, she was so scared.

Then Mary said, "You've got the key pinned on your clothes somewhere. You want to give it to me, or do I go ahead and cut away your clothes till I find it? Or if you hid it some place, maybe you better tell me."

Callie gasped and said, "It's pinned to my corset cover. Let me get it!"

Mary stepped back a little, and Callie fumbled around down inside her shirtwaist and unpinned the key.

She gave it to Old Man Beasley, and the three of us stood there while he walked over and unlocked the pawn room.

He moved things around for a while, then he came out and said, "That big squash-blossom necklace, half the bow guards, and the concha belts, and I don't know what else."

He came over to us and said, "Where you got it hid, Callie?"

She didn't answer him. She turned to me, still sniffling, and said, "I never! Link, I didn't take them!"

Mary said, "I'll take her into her room. She'll tell me!"

Callie squawked, "Link! Don't let her! Link!"

"Take her along, Mary!" I said.

Mary wasn't bluffing, and Callie knew it. Callie said, "I'll show you."

When we went outside, Franklin Yazzie and his wife were there. Their team was hitched to the wagon, but I guess when they saw Mary come in earlier, they knew something might happen, and stayed to see the fireworks.

The stuff Callie stole was in a coffee crate under a pile of sheepskins in the warehouse – necklaces and silver belts and bracelets and bow guards, the pick of the pawn jewelry. Beasley said it was all there. I carried the box into the bull pen and he hung the stuff in the pawn room. Callie didn't look ashamed or anything, she just looked sorry she didn't get away with it.

I was surprised how gentle Beasley was with her. He didn't rant and rave at her or call her a thief, he just said, "You pack your things tonight, Callie. Tomorrow, Franklin will drive you wherever you want, and put you on the train."

She said, "I've got no place to go. I haven't got anything. Not a cent." Then she turned to me, "Link, you're not going to let him . . .", but she didn't finish, because I guess she could see I wasn't going to help her. I turned away.

Beasley said, "Wait a minute," and went into his room, and in a minute or two he came out and gave her some money. He said, "There's a hundred dollars. Now, where you want to go? Gallup? Back to Prescott?"

She didn't even say thanks. She just said, "Prescott, I guess."

Then Beasley said to Yazzie, "Take my wagon and team, first thing in the mornin'. You can load blankets and water and food tonight. Take her all the way to Flagstaff. She can take the Santa Fe to Williams, and change for Prescott. You watch her get on, so we'll know she's gone. That's two hundred some miles, so I won't look for you back for two weeks or more. Take your wife along if you want."

Callie went into her room and shut the door.

Beasley went into his room and laid down.

Three Navajo women came in to buy something, so I didn't get any chance to talk to Mary, because she waited on them. So I went down to the corral and fed all the horses, and when I came back, she was getting supper. I took her by the arm and said, "Look, I've got to talk to you."

She just pulled loose, not hard, or like she was mad or anything, and said, "Supper's ready. So wash up, if you're going to. Call her when you come out. I'll get the old man."

I washed and combed my hair and came out, and when I called Callie she didn't answer. She didn't come out and eat. The three of us didn't say very much.

I thought Mary was going to stay in the hogan where she often did, so when she said, "Link, you do up the dishes, will you?" I said, "Sure."

I was glad to see her go out, because I could go out there later and talk to her. I didn't have any doubts any more. I knew what I wanted . . . I wanted her. And not for just a few nights in bed, I wanted to marry her.

I was wiping out the sink and hanging the dish rag up to dry, when I heard the wagon moving out. I ran through the bull pen and outside, and she was driving away. I yelled at her and ran after her, but she whipped the horses into a trot. I was pretty sad and discouraged. I figured I might as well go tomorrow, too. I didn't have any idea where

I'd go – for sure, not back to Prescott – but I couldn't stay here any more.

It was a warm night for that time of year, and I shucked off my long johns and got into bed naked. I thought I'd be wallowing around and not get to sleep. But the next thing I knew, someone was whispering in my ear, and saying, "Wake up! Move over!" and it was Callie, just as naked as me, crawling in with me.

She did that once before, and it was the first step toward setting me up for murder. I'd've been just as happy to have a rabid coyote cuddling up to me.

She got her arms around me and one leg over mine, and said, "Link, it doesn't have to be any different than we planned back in Prescott. You got your money back, and you can buy the place now, and I'll stay here and run it with you."

She tried to kiss me. I turned my head, got one arm between us, and pushed her away. I said, "You get out of here!"

It was like she hadn't heard me. She squirmed against me, and said, "I've got no place to go, Link. I've got nobody. I'll be good to you. You don't know how good I can be to somebody I like." And she went on like that day after Ruby Blair beat her up and left her, right here in this same room . . .

how she couldn't help it, Ruby made her, and all that again.

It all made me sick, and I said, "Shut up! Get the hell out of here, or I'll throw you out!"

Well, that shut her up, all right. For a minute. Then she jumped out of bed and screeched at me loud enough to wake the dead. She was sputtering and spitting. She yelled, "It's that black Indian slut, isn't it, you dirty Indian lover! You dirty, cheap, murdering Indian lover! Well let me tell you, you murdered my Ruby! You murdered my husband! And we've got friends, Link! Don't think we haven't, Ruby and me! Down in Prescott! Friends that won't just forget you killed him!"

She went on ranting, and I got out of bed and opened the door and pushed her into the hall. She dug in her heels, pushing back, and kept yelling at me over her shoulder, "Harry Peters! I'll tell Harry Peters! He won't just let it go! He's a friend of mine! You didn't know that, did you, Linkie! I used to sleep with Harry! Every time Ruby went out of town, I slept with Harry! Didn't know that, either, did you! Well, I'll tell Harry, and Harry will come up here and kill you! And her, too, if I tell him to!"

She ran out of breath, and just then Old

Man Beasley came out of his room in his underwear, holding up a lamp. She looked half crazy, with her hair tangled around her face, and a wild look in her eyes. She said, real quiet this time, "Harry'll kill you, Link! For me! And for himself, too, because he hates your guts!"

She didn't try to cover up or anything, just walked straight toward the old man, and turned in at her room and shut the door.

Beasley said, "Well, hell is only half the fury of a scorned woman. That's the exact words that's in the Bible, Link. You know, it ain't Ruby that's botherin' her, nor not gettin' your money away from you ... it's 'cause you'd rather have Mary than her."

"Yeah," I said. "I kind of got that idea." And I went back to bed.

Well, I didn't leave the next day. I couldn't quite give up the hope that Mary would come and I could straighten things out with her. I didn't understand her, and I never would, I suppose. I knew she didn't trust any white man except Old Man Beasley, and this wasn't just because of what had happened to her when she tried to live in a city like any white girl. It was the whole Navajo part of her. None of them trusted white men, and they had plenty of good reasons not to, reasons even to hate all white men, I suppose.

268

But I couldn't see where, as far as she was concerned, I was just another white-eyes, a sort of a standard sample of all white men. I was Link Conway, and it had taken me a long time to come to it, or to realize I had come to it, but I loved her. She wasn't stupid . . . and Indians know pretty much all about you without being told, what kind of a man you are. She had to know I wasn't a bad man, and that what happened down there in the canyon the day before I left, and that night, had to happen between a woman and a man in the setup we were in, just like the sun had to rise every day, and nobody could stop it. And if she was going to be honest with herself, it wasn't all me, not by a long shot, especially that second time. So it had to be that it was the Indian half of her, just the deep-down, born-in instinct of an Indian to forever distrust any and all white men. It sure wasn't fair to me. Unless, maybe, she just plain didn't like me . . . and I was almost sure that wasn't true.

So I hung around. I thought about going to Canyon de Chelly to see her, to argue with her, but I had my pride, too. And not only that, I didn't want to go through a lot more insults and unfair remarks, and maybe another slap in the face. What I kept hoping was that, alone down there, she'd find out she was lonesome now, even if she hadn't ever been before, and she'd realize I had actually been pretty damn nice to her all that time, and would come to see that I really loved her. Then, too, I figured that maybe the whole trouble was that I never actually came right out and asked her to marry me, because I hadn't really been sure. But then, she'd heard me say I would, that day in the bull pen when Callie was saying all those nasty things about her.

The Navajos began to come back to trade. I guess they were getting used to the idea that I wasn't a ghost, and I guess they all knew, the way they get to know things, that I had been with Mary all that time down in Canyon de Chelly. Anyway, I did everything I could to keep busy, and while I wasn't much interested any more, I was learning a lot about the business in spite of myself. I guess that encouraged Old Man Beasley to think I was still going to buy him out, and finally, after another week, he asked me.

"God damn it, boy," he said, "You're givin' me a bad time! I wish t'God, if you're gonna buy the place, you'd do it an' not keep things danglin'. I sent a letter out with Yazzie to the superintendent over at Fort Defiance about transferrin' the license to you, an' I oughta hear any day now. But there won't be no trouble there. You was all hot to buy when you come, an' now I don't know what the hell's got into you."

I didn't have any answer for him, and I had about quit being hopeful. I said, "Yeah, I know it ain't fair. I'll leave in the morning. I'm sorry it turned out this way for you."

Well, next morning, I heard him stirring around before daylight, the way he did sometimes, banging the coffee pot, and shaking the ashes down in the cook stove. His rheumatism had got a lot better with the beginning of spring, and he was naturally an early riser when he felt good.

I went back to sleep, but I got up about seven, shaved and got dressed, and began to pack my blanket roll and check over my saddlebags. Suddenly I realized there wasn't any more noise from the kitchen. I went out there, and there was a note speared on a fork stuck in the sugar bowl, where I'd be sure to see it. It said:

It is two weeks since Yazzie took her to the train and he ought to be back in two three days now. You dont have to open the place. Just dont unlock, and dont let no navvys in. Yazzie can open when he gits back. I have went to see Mary and talk some sence into her. I guess she dont see that if she dont show some sence you will not buy from me and that will be a dirty trick on me after all I done for her.

Well, what could I do? I couldn't just ride off and leave with nobody minding the place. Besides, I couldn't help but think that he might talk her into coming back. I left the door locked and didn't answer the few Navajos that came, and the day after that, Franklin Yazzie drove in with his wife.

First thing he said when he got down from the wagon was, "She din't go to Prescott. She make me stop at station an' she send telegram to somebody. I can't see who it is. Then she say take her to the Weatherford Hotel, and I say she gotta take train to Prescott. That's what Mr. Beasley said. She swear at me, right there on the street, call me dirty name an' everybody lookin' at us. An' she say, 'God damn you, you gonna drive me to hotel?', so I take her there, an' she get room, an' carry her suitcase an' carpetbag up to room. You better tell Mr. Beasley it ain't my fault."

"Well, it ain't," I said. "He'll see that."

Yazzie opened for business the next day, and I just hung around, doing nothing, waiting for Old Man Beasley to come back to see if he'd got anywhere arguing with Mary.

I didn't really expect he would.

Three days later, about the middle of the morning, I was down in the corral checking Sox's shoes. I hadn't made up my mind whether I'd ride down into Canyon de Chelly myself, for one last try to talk some sense into Mary. I was sick of hanging around with nothing happening, and nothing settled, and I was going to leave for sure, this time. I guess it was settled, as far as she was concerned, but I just couldn't accept it without seeing her once more, having her tell me to my face.

Two people came riding over the hill and down the road to the post, and one of them dragging a pack horse. The horses were no good, just crow bait, and I didn't recognize her until they were within a hundred yards or so. It was Callie, wearing pants and a Mackinaw, and looking miserable, humped over in the saddle like she'd never been on a horse before. It took me another minute to recognize Harry Peters, and then it was too late. I wasn't packing my gun, and they were right at the door of the post, now. For a minute, I thought I'd climb onto Sox bareback and make a run for it, but they saw me, and Harry already had his carbine out of the boot. He hollered, "Come on up here, Link!"

I came out, closed the corral gate and

started to walk up to them. Franklin Yazzie came running out of the door and cut for the guest hogan where he lived, going like a boogered jackrabbit.

Callie yelled, and her horse spooked and r'ared up. Harry Peters swung around and took a snap shot at Yazzie, but he was too late. Yazzie went diving around the middle hogan, where the door was, out of sight from us. Callie's horse pitched, and she was screaming and hanging onto the saddle horn, and Peters caught it by the cheek strap and held it. He said, "Chris' sakes, Callie, can't you hold this God damn animal?"

He got off his own horse and turned to me, where I was walking up to them. I guess he already saw I wasn't packing a gun, because he didn't threaten me or point the carbine at me. He just said, "Come on inside, Link, and we'll find that money."

I had my money in the money belt, under my shirt, because I'd figured on riding out today. I said, "Well, Harry, you're too late. I bought the place from Old Man Beasley. Paid him off, every cent I had, and he's long gone."

He started to say something, and Callie said, "Harry! What's the matter with you! Yazzie might have a gun in that hogan!"

He said, "Hell, he's just went for cover like

a gopher. I know these Navvies. They got no nerve."

"But, Harry . . . !"

He handed her the carbine. She didn't want to take it, but he shoved it into her hand. "Here, it's ready to go. Just pull the trigger. If he shows his nose outside that hogan, take a shot at him."

He pulled his six-gun out of the holster, and handed her the reins of his horse. He said, "Here, hang on to this plug, too, while I take Link inside."

She looked scared, but she looped the reins over her arm. Their miserable pack horse was tied to Harry Peter's saddle horn with about fifteen feet of lead rope. Harry should've known better. Tying to the saddle horn, and too much lead rope, why that's just plain suicide for a packer.

"You go ahead, Link. We'll have a look in that hole in your bedroom wall, first." Then he changed his mind, and said, "First, though, why don't you just peel your clothes off? Maybe you got it stuck in your boot, or in a money belt."

"You mean right here?"

"You bashful or something? Come on, get started."

Then Callie said, "Harry, we've got to hurry. We don't know where Beasley is! He's around somewhere, and he must have heard that shot. Link never carried that money on him! He hid it some place. Hurry up, will you?" She looked all around the horizon, worried and scared.

"Well, you heard her," Peters said to me. "Jump!" And he jabbed the muzzle of his Colt's into my kidneys so hard I yelled.

Callie said, "You better step lively, you dirty Indian humper! I told you I'd get Harry!"

I started to walk inside, and he shoved the gun between my shoulders hard, and said, "Hurry it up!"

Inside, I almost ran. I thought I might get into my room and grab my carbine leaning in the corner, before he came in, but he wasn't going to be caught by any move like that. He stayed right at my back, and when we were in the room, he made me sit on the bed with my back to him, and he handed me my carbine and said, "Shuck out all the shells, Link! Just in case you should manage to get your hands on it before we're through." So I did, and laid the carbine on the bed.

Then he backed off, keeping me covered, and picked my Colt's out of the holster where I had it hung on my saddle, in a corner. He stuck it in the back of his belt.

"Now," he said, "I know all about that

little hidey-hole in the wall. Pull the bed out, and take the loose brick out."

"It ain't there, Harry. I told you. Beasley got it all."

"Well, he must've give you a receipt, or a bill of sale, or something. So if it ain't in that hole behind the bed, then you show me the receipt, and we'll see what happens next."

I pulled the bed out and showed him the empty hiding place.

"All right, Link. We'll go look at that receipt. Where's it at?"

"Well," I said, and I was thinking fast and not getting any ideas, "he . . . well, he had to have it registered or authorized or something, over at Fort Defiance, so the Bureau'll know that . . ."

He kicked me below the knee, and I almost fell down. "That's enough. Don't waste my time no more. Get me that money, or I shoot you. You know me, Link. You know I'll do it!"

"Why should I? You ain't gonna shoot me till you get the money, else how will you find it?"

"You'll show me, or if you're hurt too bad to show me, you'll tell me. 'Cause if I shoot both your knee caps off, and you still hold out, then I'll shoot you through both elbows."

And he reached out and ripped the front

sight of his pistol across my face, and if I hadn't jumped back, it would have torn across my left eye.

"So quit foolin' around, Link. Where's it at?"

And I remembered where it was. Not the money. I knew where that was, all right, and I knew as soon as he had it he'd kill me. No, I remembered where something was I needed a lot more right now than ten million dollars.

"All right, if I've got your word you won't kill me."

"Why, Link! What would I want to do that for? Not just because you cheated the Development Land and Cattle Company on that deal for your section? And sure not just because you caught me by surprise in the Palace Bar, and cracked my jaw and loosened my teeth. No, Link, I was kind of mad at first, and that's why I took that shot at you on Mingus Mountain . . . that, and I wanted your money. Don't know how I come to miss you."

"I didn't know whether that was you or Ruby Blair, but I promised I'd pay that slug back to whoever put it in the cantle of my saddle. I will, too, Harry, if you don't ride out right now. I promise you, Harry!"

"You ain't gonna have the time or the chance, Link. In fact, you've run clean out of time as of this minute! Now where is it?"

"It's under the counter, out in the bull pen."

"For God sakes! Under the counter! You simple in the head? With all them Navvies, an' that old man around all the time?"

"He's got a lot of junk under there, in old paper sacks, just helter-skelter. A busted alarm clock, and an old pair of spurs with one rowel gone, and a couple cigar boxes of bolts and screws . . . just a lot of junk nobody'd ever think to look at. Especially anybody looking for anything valuable, because everybody knows I'd never put my money in a paper sack under the counter."

"Maybe you're right," he said. "Let's go see."

So he marched me down the hall and into the bull pen, with the gun in my back, and stepped in right behind me when I went behind the counter.

I bent over with my back to him, and it was dark behind the counter, and darker on that shelf under the counter. That's where Beasley kept his bundles of paper sacks . . . and that's where he kept that old single-action Colt's .45, in an innocent looking, crumpled, old, paper sack . . . out of sight but close to hand. At least, that's where he told me he kept it, the day Ruby robbed me and knocked him down with his gun.

It was there. I could feel it. I got my hand inside the big sack, and got a good grip on it. But Harry had his gun right in my back, pushing against me. His was full cocked, and the one in my hand inside that sack wasn't. And when I cocked it, it would click, and he'd kill me. Well, I had to make my try ... because money or not, he was going to kill me.

And outside. Callie yelled, "Harry! He's coming!"

Harry swore, and straightened up with a jerk and half turned to look out the front door.

I didn't try to take the pistol out of the bag, I just pulled it out from under the shelf and cocked it as I swung it at Harry.

He heard it, and he knew. He twisted sideways and tried to bring his Colt's to bear and I shot him in the chest. Before he crumpled I cocked and shot him again. He fired, too, but not till he was falling, and his gun pointing at the floor. My ears were ringing, and my eyes burning with the smoke.

Outside, Callie screamed, and I heard a shot. I jumped over Harry Peters' body and ran for the door, and I heard horses squealing and hoofs thumping. The three horses were all tangled up in reins and the lead rope, bucking and pitching, and Callie down under them on the ground, with her left foot hung in the stirrup.

Twenty feet away, Franklin Yazzie was standing gawking, with a carbine in his hands. Then he jumped into the middle of the milling horses the same time I did, and while we were in the middle of that tangle grabbing reins and yelling at the horses, I heard another yell up the hill. There was a rattle of hubs, clash of iron tires, and the pound of hoofs as a wagon came rattling and skidding down the hill.

I kicked a horse's leg, hit another on the nose with my fist, and got Callie by one arm. Yazzie was flailing around with his carbine, and managed to hammer the horses back from me, as I dragged her clear. When I picked her up, her head just flopped loose. I ran inside, and laid her on a stack of rugs. I put my ear to her chest, but my own heart was pounding so hard I couldn't tell if hers was running.

Yazzie came in and said, "Jesus God! I got my carbine an' I couldn't find no shells. And when I did find 'em an' got loaded an' crawl out on my belly, she see me, an' she yell for that man. An' then come those two shots inside, an' her horse start jumpin', an' her gun went off. I don't know if she shot at me, or just shot it off by accident. An' all three horses pitchin' an' tangle up in lead rope, an' she fall off."

Old Man Beasley came in, looking scared. It was his wagon I'd heard coming down the hill. He didn't say anything, but when I laid Callie on the stack of Navajo blankets, he held her hand and said, "Callie? Callie girl?" She couldn't hear anything.

We had them both in Beasley's wagon. Harry Peters' body wrapped up in a tarp and Callie lying with her head the other way. She was alive, but still unconscious, and her color was bad. There was a trickle of blood out of one nostril that wouldn't stop, and she coughed once in a while, and bloody froth would show on her lips.

The old man said it wasn't fitting that I should do it, but Yazzie's wife wouldn't go anywhere near her, so I had to undress her and get her into a nightgown and robe. We made a soft place for her in the wagon with sheepskins and blankets. There was only one thing to do – get her to Fort Defiance to a doctor as soon as we could. And Chinle was thirty miles and Fort Defiance another forty-five. We'd never make it tonight . . . maybe late tomorrow if we half killed the horses.

Beasley and I had to put Harry in the wagon without any help from Yazzie because he was deathly afraid of a dead man. But he said he didn't mind cleaning up the blood and mess where I'd cut Harry down, and would stay and run the post. We'd be gone several days at least, because there'd sure be some kind of investigation at Fort Defiance.

When we started, about noon, Old Man Beasley rode up on the seat with me, but he kept twisting around to look back at Callie, and asking me to stop so he could get back there and feel her pulse. Finally I said, "Get down there with her, why don't you?" And he did.

Next time I looked around, he had her head in his lap, and he was smoothing out her forehead with his horny, old hand. He looked up at me and said, "I don't think she's gonna make it, Link." I could hear her breathing, even over the rattle of hubs and tug chains. It was loud, kind of like snoring.

"You should of seen her when she was little, Link. She used to climb up on my lap and pull my whiskers . . . and she'd come to me, later, when that son of a bitch took the strap to her, and crawl into my arms and cry, and I'd pat her on the head and give her candy and wish I had the guts to shoot the bastard. You know, I never got married, I never had no kids, and she, well she kind of was like my own kid. Only when she begin to run wild, I'd get awful mad at her. I been mad at her a thousand times, Link. Why, she even pulled things on me. Got so I couldn't really trust her. But I always kept it in mind that he done that to her. It wasn't never really her fault, even though she turned out pretty bad, I guess. But, Link, you got your money back. You shouldn't hold no grudge. You just should've knowed her back when she was little."

"Yeah, and then of course, she never set you up for murder, and helped steal your last cent from you."

"Why, that Ruby, he like to killed me with that gun. I was in it just like you was."

"Oh, no. You just happened to get in the way. They weren't after you, but they tried to kill me, old man!"

So we slugged along, hour after hour, planning to stop at Sam Day's post in Chinle for something to eat and a couple hours sleep. It got dark, and we still had two or three miles to go, and Beasley stood up in the wagon and said, "Link, stop, will you? I . . . I think she's goin'." He was sniffling, and wiping his nose on his sleeve. "Her breathing, it kind of stops, then goes again."

"Light the lantern," I said. He fumbled around finding it, got it lit and hung it from a nail in the middle wagon bow. Meantime, I stopped the team, and got into the back with them. I had to stoop under the wagon cover, and Beasley had her head in his lap again. He said, "Listen, Link. Listen to her breathing. What you think?"

I knelt down and put my head down close. It would sound like she wasn't breathing at all, and I'd think she was gone. Then she'd start up again, hoarse and kind of loud. I did feel sorry for her, then. She had been so pretty and smart, and one time I'd been crazy about her. The old man was right. She sure wasn't born vicious, and I guess maybe she wasn't really responsible for what she had turned into. And I guess, too, twisted as it was, she had really loved Ruby Blair. At least, I couldn't figure out how she'd do the things she did for him if she didn't love him.

All of a sudden her eyes were open, looking up at me, those big blue eyes, sort of vague and wandering. But she knew me. "Link? I'm sorry, Link. I'm really sorry!"

I choked up and took her hand. "Well, Callie, let's call bygones bygones. Don't worry about it."

She laid quiet for a minute with her eyes shut, then opened them again and looked up at me, and kind of whispered because she couldn't get her breath very good, "Yes, I'm sorry, Link. I'm sorry Ruby didn't shoot your filthy Indian-loving heart out of you. I wish I could see you dead before I go." And she smiled – a sweet, gentle smile – and settled back. I got up and climbed out of the wagon.

In a few minutes, Beasley said, "I think . . . well, I think she's gone, Link."

There was nothing we could do. I got up on the seat, and we pushed on. We got to Sam Day's Chinle post and woke him up. Sam built up his kitchen fire and made coffee and got a meal for us. He said we'd ought to get on our way before daylight, because if the Navvies came around early in the morning and found out there were two bodies in the wagon, they'd scatter like so many boogered quail and not come back for days.

Beasley said, "Just leave us lay down for a couple of hours." Then he said to me, "Link, can I talk to you?"

I said, "Sure," and we went out into Sam Day's bull pen and lit a lamp and sat on a stack of rugs.

The old man said, "I changed Mary's mind for her. She's gonna marry you. At least, she'll run the post for you. I don't know how strong she is for gettin' married. None of 'em bother, unless the missionaries have got to 'em."

Something funny began to happen in my chest, like a kind of warm light spreading

286

through me. "She told you she would?" I said. "Why didn't she say something to me?"

"Well, she didn't exactly say so," he said, "but I got a damn good hunch."

"Hunch!" I said, and that warm light went out.

"So," he said, "I could tell 'em the whole story at Fort Defiance, get the two of 'em buried, an' all that, an' you wouldn't have to go there at all, right now. You can go find her. I'll find out what red tape I gotta go through to transfer the license to you, an' then go on to Gallup an' sell the team an' wagon an' catch me a train for Californy. If you'd trust me to send you the bill of sale. If you'll pay me now."

We heard a horse come pounding up the road and pull in at the hitchrack. Then Mary came in . . . and it's a funny thing, but I knew it was her before she got inside.

She came straight to me and put her hands on my shoulders and asked, "You didn't get shot?"

I grabbed her hands and stood up. I said, "No. I'm all right. But I killed Harry Peters, and Callie got stomped by the horses. She's dead, too."

Mary leaned her head on my chest and said, "I heard you and some man shot each other, and Mr. Beasley took you in the wagon and

287

started for Fort Defiance. I rode as fast as I could."

Beasley slapped me on the back and said, "Guess that shows you, Link! 'Cause if she'd do that, why . . ."

"Get out of here!" I yelled at him. When he went out, I said, "Mary, I'll put it to you straight, once and for all. Are you going to marry me?"

"Yes," she said.

Well, I couldn't say anything, I was so surprised. I reached out for her and held her against my chest. For a minute there, that's all there was in my world . . . Mary Wilson . . . Adezhbah . . . in my arms.

She pushed at me and said, "You're squashing me!"

"Well, I guess I oughta leave well enough alone and not ask any questions," I said, "but what changed your mind?"

"Mr. Beasley did," she said. "He's got a very practical mind. He reminded me of all the things he's done for me, like my own father . . . and he really has, Link, he's been wonderful to me. Then he said he couldn't imagine me being so ungrateful I wouldn't marry you, because if I didn't you wouldn't buy him out, and he'd die of rheumatism and I'd always have it on my conscience."

"Well," I said, "I guess I shouldn't look a

gift horse in the teeth, but if I was pressed, I could come up with some better reasons than that to get married."

"So now I'm a horse!" she said, and turned her face up to be kissed . . . and I did. I kissed her good.

She said, when I let her go, "Some ways you're a fool, Link. That day you rode out of the canyon, I was afraid to come out of the hogan, because I knew I'd go running after you. It almost killed me to have you go, and if you had even turned to look back . . . ! And my wonderful, warm hogan was the emptiest, coldest place in the world that night."

"Well then," I said, "for God's sake, why . . ."

And she broke in and said, "I was afraid. I've got half white blood, Link, but I'm Navajo. I'm Indian. And you're white. And I couldn't trust you. I couldn't bring myself to gamble, to risk a year or two, or maybe only a week or two, and then you getting tired of me, and of the reservation, tired of being a squaw man . . ."

Then I broke in. "Listen, don't call me that! I don't like that word! You'll be my wife, not my squaw!"

She said, "But you never said . . . you never did tell me that . . ." She couldn't seem to say

289

it, but I knew what she meant.

"I do," I said, "I love you, all the way. Maybe I won't say it to you very often, because it just ain't in me to use words like that. But I mean it, and you remember I mean it, from now on out."

"Me, too, Link," she said. "And I know what you mean. I can't say it easy, either."

"What really changed your mind?" I asked her.

"The old man did," she said. "I laughed at him when he said I owed it to him to marry you. But then he asked me something that I should have thought of a long time ago. He said, 'Have you forgot your father and mother? Have you forgot he was a Belecana, a white-eyes? You ever stop to think maybe you've got the chance to have the same thing with Link your mother had with your father? You'll be a damn fool to throw it away.' Well, one thing I'm not is a damn fool, Link."

"I ain't so sure," I said. "Come on inside. We've got some business to do."

Well, I paid Old Man Beasley five thousand dollars cash, right there in Sam Day's kitchen, and he wrote out a bill of sale and Day signed it as witness.

When I stuck it in my wallet, the old man said, "Them people at Fort Defiance have knowed me a long time. I'll fix up about the

290

license, and tell them exactly what happened. I don't doubt there'll be an investigation, but you got me for a witness, and Franklin Yazzie, and Mary, and don't worry about it."

"Well, what about Ruby Blair," I said. "I've got no witnesses there, except Mary, and she was involved in it."

"That's the best part of it," Beasley said. "No witnesses at all. And nobody's gonna dig him up from under all that rock, even if anybody found out. Don't tell nobody! Sure, the Navvies know about it, but they don't care which white-eyes kills which other one. If it ever comes down to it, you just play ignorant, and your wife can't testify against you. Even if Sam, here, or me was to say anything, what do we know? We wasn't there, so, unless your conscience bothers you, I'd forget it. What do you say, Sam?"

"I say the same," Sam said. "Forget it. Everybody else will."

"Well, my conscience sure doesn't bother," I said.

Then Mary said, "Sam, can we borrow another horse? We better be heading back then, if Mr. Beasley doesn't need us to go with him.

"No, I don't need you at Fort Defiance," Beasley said, "and Franklin Yazzie don't need you at Ram House Post, neither, not for a week or so. Sam can send him word you won't be back for a while."

"Well, hell," Sam Day said. "Where would they go, this time of year? We could get another snow any day, or . . ."

I grabbed Mary's hand and pulled her toward the door. "Come on," I said, "Sox can carry double, as far as we're going."

She said, "Wait! Hold on a minute!" and I let go.

She kissed Old Man Beasley square on the mouth in the middle of that tangle of whiskers, and said something in Navajo.

He patted her on the shoulder, and said, "You're a nice girl, Adezhbah," and he wiped his nose with his bandana, and blinked at her, and said, "You run along, now."

It was all down hill, and her hundred pounds and my hundred and seventy weren't too much load for Sox. We let him walk down that long grade, with the cliffs getting higher and higher on both sides of us. The one on the north rim was as black as ink, and the south side silvery with moonlight . . . down past Junction Rock, where Ruby Blair stood off the Navajo posse, and where I jumped him . . . and on past where he shot me down. Then along the flat, wet sand, splashing through the shallow creek, under the pale gleam of White House Ruin in its niche in that God-awful, vertical sweep of cliff – we turned to ride across to our hogan. The dog came yammering out, and Mary yelled at him in Navajo and he shut up. Her team whinnied from the corral.

She slid down from behind me, and I got off. I said, "Mary, maybe you want to wait for a preacher. I can go back to Ram House and we can send word for one, and you come out when he shows up."

"The Navajo half of me doesn't need a preacher, and the Belecana half can just be patient! But one thing, let's get it straight right at the start. You marry into the Dineh, you've got a lot to learn, and you better toe the mark! For instance, it's the woman that runs the house and owns the sheep, the rugs, and all the household stuff. And you just step out of line once, and I can get rid of you. All I have to do is put your saddle outside the door, and you're through."

I thought that over while I led Sox into the corral and unsaddled him. I hung the saddle on the fence and came back to her.

"Have you got a couple of big spikes?" I said.

"Spikes? What for?"

"I'm gonna spike that saddle to the rafters

where you can't ever reach it!"

"Good! I'll help you!"

I grabbed her and kissed her again, and said, "Old Belecana custom. I'm supposed to carry you over the door sill!" I grabbed her around the waist and under the knees, and swung her off the ground. We were both laughing, and I hugged her to me as tight as I could.

I said, "Hey, one question. Very important. Which half of you is the Navajo half I can sleep with till we get a preacher?"

"Why, it's the top half of me," she said. "Maybe you better go sleep by yourself in the wagon again!"

"Not till we have our next fight," I said, and carried her to the hogan.

She reached down and took the peg out of the hasp, pulling the door open. I carried her inside.

The publishers hope that this book has given you enjoyable reading. Large Print Books are specially designed to be as easy to see and hold as possible. If you wish a complete list of our books, please ask at your local library or write directly to: Curley Publishing, Inc., P.O. Box 37, South Yarmouth, Massachusetts, 02664.